DEATH VISITS CANAAN

Also by Edwin D. Michael

A Valley Called Canaan: 1885-2002

Shadow of the Alleghenies

DEATH visits CANAAN

A
first-person account
of life in the Canaan Wilderness
during 1880,
as conveyed
to Edwin D. Michael
by Georgie S. Leatherman

quarrier
press

Charleston, West Virginia

First Edition

10 9 8 7 6 5 4 3 2 1

Printed in United States of America

Library of Congress Control Number: 2011944284
ISBN-13: 978-1-891852-81-7
ISBN-10: 1-891852-81-7

Cover illustration: L. Jason Queen
Book design: Mark S. Phillips

All persons mentioned in this novel existed in real life. However, the majority of
the day-to-day activities described herein are fictional. For a list of the documented
historical events that formed the framework for this novel please see the List of
Chronological Events on page 160.

This historical novel depicts one person's interpretation of the documents
referencing George S. Leatherman's life. Other individuals have construed the
historical writings differently.

For a detailed history of the George W. Leatherman family, please see the article
"Researching the Leatherman Stone" written by Elaine George and published
in the October, 2011, issue of *Chronicles of the Tucker County Highlands History and
Education Project*, Davis, WV 26260.

Distributed by:

West Virginia Book Company
1125 Central Avenue
Charleston, WV 25302
www.wvbookco.com

Contents

DEDICATION

This historical novel is dedicated to my mother, Isolene Gump Michael, who personally helped settle one small area of West Virginia—Plum Run in Marion County. Her never-wavering confidence in my knowledge and ability was the incentive that kept me sitting at the computer for days, months, and years until the manuscript was sent to the printer.

ACKNOWLEDGMENTS

I will forever be indebted to those many persons who provided advice, encouragement, and historical information during the years this novel was being prepared. Julie Dzaack and Elaine George contributed numerous facts regarding the history of various Leathermans who resided in Mineral and Tucker counties. Frank Jernejcic provided invaluable stream maps of the Potomac and Blackwater drainages. Several individuals graciously edited early drafts, including: Norm Julian, Julie Dzaack, Ken Dzaack, and my wife, Jane.

Residents Of Canaan Valley In 1880 According To 1880 Census

It is impossible to determine from the 1880 U.S. Census the families that lived within what is now known as Canaan Valley. Canaan Valley was in the Dry Fork District, but the name, "Canaan Valley", was not entered into the 1880 U.S. Census records. Hu Maxwell, in his 1884 book "History of Tucker County", stated that five families lived in Canaan Valley: Solomon Cosner, Robert Eastman, James Freeland, George Leatherman, and John Nine. Individuals living at these residences, with actual spellings as listed in the 1880 U.S. Census, are as follows:

Solomon, W., 53 years old, farmer.
    (This was almost definitely Solomon Cosner)
Catherine, 53 years old, wife.
Ameil, 21 years old, son.
Freeling H. 19 years old, son.
Commodore P., 16 years old, son.
Ulyssus, S. G., 14 years old, son.
Abraham, 12 years old, son.
Stephen D., 9 years old, son.
Warness, A. C. 46 years old, boarder.
Kallogg, John. 53 years old, boarder.
Shell, Almeda A., 20 years old, laborer.
Cosner, C. C. 27 years old, son.
Mary J., 24 years old, CC Cosner's wife.

Eastham, Robert W., 38 years old, gentleman.
Mary, 36 years old, wife.

Freeling, James, 75 years old, farmer.
(This was almost certainly James Freeland)
Isaac, 36 years old, son of James, farmer.
Manerva, 35 years old, wife of Isaac.
Rebecca, 13 years old, daughter of Isaac.
Margaret V. 11 years old, daughter of Isaac.

Leatherman, George, 44 years old, farmer.
Caroline, 31 years old, wife.
Warner W., 20 years old, son.
John W., 18 years old, son.
Zedekiah, 13 years old, son.
Mary, 11 years old, daughter.
George S. 9 years old, son.
Daniel R., 4 years old, son.
Emma M. 2 years old, daughter.

Nine, John, 47 years old, farmer.
Margaret, 42 years old, wife.
Arlettis A., 20 years old, son.
George W. 14 years old, son.
John Athford, 13 years old, son.
Isadora, 11 years old, daughter.
James, H. H. 6 years old, son.
Angeline, 3 years old, daughter.
Erra C. 11/12 years old, son.
Edward S. Cosner, 2 years old, grandson.

CHAPTER ONE

The Boy's Spirit

Shortly after my uneventful birth in a sturdy log cabin nestled within the rugged mountains of West Virginia I was christened, George Sandford Leatherman. After fewer than ten wonderful, exciting years on this good earth my slender, damaged body was laid to rest in a shallow grave in the Canaan Valley wilderness. The hand-chiseled inscription on my rough gravestone read, "G. S. L., Died Dec. 5, 1880, Age 9 Yr & 211 Da".

My ageless spirit has effortlessly roamed the Canaan landscape surrounding my final resting place for over one hundred years, as it will for the next one hundred, and the next one hundred after that, until I transmigrate to another earthly body. When I once again inhabit a living being I will have no memory of my previous life.

At first it didn't trouble me that my full name was not on the gravestone. But after one hundred years I became concerned that my human person, George S. Leatherman, the boy, was doomed to anonymity. As the early settlers of Canaan Valley—Cosners, Nines, Freelands, and Easthams—faded away, so did knowledge of my person and my grave.

Few people living at the end of the twentieth century were aware of my isolated gravestone, and only a handful had ever seen it. No other gravestones are in the area, and few signs of human habitation remain around what was our Canaan homestead. If a tree, or even a large tree limb, should fall on my gravestone it would pass into oblivion, never to be seen by human eyes again.

Although my family did not reside long in the Canaan Valley wilderness, we deserve some small recognition for the role we played in the settlement of this unique area. My gravestone would function as such a monument—if the public knew of its existence and knew the full name of the person the initials, G. S. L., represented. Unfortunately, the dead often pass into oblivion and leave not a trace of their life on this earth.

Spirits cannot alter the predestined events of human lives, but we can modify the daily behavior of a few living individuals in small, relatively insignificant ways. During the 130 years I have been George Sandford Leatherman's spirit, only seven unique individuals were receptive to my transmissions. Six were early residents who lived and worked in the remote corner of Canaan Valley where my primitive gravestone is firmly anchored.

With my guidance, a logger found a black obsidian Shawnee spear point, a young girl discovered an orphaned red fox pup, a woodsman found an axe he dropped while crossing the Blackwater River, a farmer found a calf that had wandered into the balsam swamp and became mired in deep muck, a mother discovered a soothing herb that stilled her newborn's incessant crying, and an elderly man remembered where he left his rifle.

The seventh individual receptive to my influence was a very special hunter who first visited the area in 1970. He seemed the ideal candidate to discover my barely-visible gravestone, identify G.S.L., and subsequently learn more about my history and my family.

Many hunters have frequented my haunts in Canaan Valley while pursuing black bear, white-tailed deer, wild turkey, wood ducks, ruffed grouse, and woodcock. Most made only one or two trips, while a few returned year after year for decades. I gradually realized there was something special about this one particular human after ten years of carefully studying his actions. He had great respect for the land, showed deep love for his dog, and was attracted to the Sand Run area where my family had solemnly dug my small grave and later placed my gravestone.

The day the hunter first responded to my thoughts was a most exciting one for me. It was an unseasonably warm October afternoon, with the sun's rays unobstructed by clouds. Both the man and his dog—Bonnie, he called her—were quite thirsty. Sand Run was running seasonably low, and not safe to drink because of its upstream beaver population. I "guided" the man to a small cold spring that flowed above ground for only a few feet before disappearing under a jumble of boulders. Although crawling white flatworms were prominent residents of the spring, the innocent invertebrates did not deter the two thirsty individuals.

During the three decades the hunter visited Sand Run, he was typically accompanied by Brittany spaniels, energetic, short-tailed hunting dogs that loved to hunt grouse and woodcock. The hunter and his dogs were close friends, enjoying one another's company while at the same time enjoying the plants and animals of Canaan Valley.

I've observed that if a dog unfailingly loves its master that human typically possesses countless other admirable qualities. I commingled ("transmelded" in spirit language) my thoughts with those of the hunter several times; once helping him find an apple tree hanging heavy with juicy, yellow fruits. Another time I directed him to a fallen red spruce tree where he and his dog found shelter from a surprise hailstorm.

On several occasions I assisted him in finding his Brittany spaniel when it was solidly on point in a dense meadowsweet thicket. Relieved from my solitude, I relished developing our rare relationship, with plans to expand it even further in the future.

A hunter makes thousands of subconscious and conscious decisions every time he enters the woods; to go around a tree on the right or the left; to step over a log or step on top of it; to duck his head and crawl under a leaning tree or skirt around it; or to direct his glance to the right or to the left. By influencing only a few of these decisions I was able to modify this particular hunter's movements on several of his trips into Canaan Valley.

Those persons who utilize all of their natural senses are the ones most likely to respond to my influence. Never have I been able to transmeld my thoughts with those of persons who relied only on their sense of sight. This hunter regularly used his sense of smell, analyzing the scents left by wild animals and the odors characterizing various plants. He would feel the bark of trees, the texture of rocks, the composition of a handful of forest litter, or the coolness of the Sand

Run waters. He never hesitated to taste blueberries, serviceberries, cranberries, chokecherries, and teaberries. He seldom refused a snack of the inner core of a cattail stem rising from the edge of a beaver pond, the oyster mushrooms growing on a dead aspen, the puffballs scattered over the forest floor, the tender tips of greenbrier, or the new leaves of birch trees and low-growing teaberry plants.

When this man was not hunting, I curiously watched him listen intently for the calls of songbirds, the drumming of grouse, the peents of breeding woodcock, and the winnowing of snipe. He counted deer droppings, searched for duck nests, and recorded the tracks left by bear, bobcat, and foxes. Although I didn't understand the purpose behind these actions, I noted he was zealous about the efforts involved.

The hunter carried a small notebook, and constantly pulled it from his coat pocket to record observations or experiences. He seemed to take great delight in even the smallest discovery. It was obvious he was driven by an intense curiosity and a love for the natural world, plus a compelling desire to be an integral part of the wonderful, complex Canaan Valley circle of life.

He appeared blessed with the spirit of inquiry, seeing and understanding what others only glimpsed—traits I considered important if he were to pursue the history of my gravestone. I was indeed fortunate to find such an individual. Spirits do not worry or regret or grieve or feel guilt. However, we do observe and feel satisfaction with certain outcomes.

It was an autumn day, with the goldenrod glistening wet and steamy from a sun-warmed frost, when I first guided the hunter to the forested hillside. There, overlooking Sand Run, my small gravestone had stood erect for over 100 years. The lichen-covered stone was only ten inches wide and eighteen inches tall, and blended well with the carpet of fallen leaves and downed treetops.

The man and his dog moved as an experienced team through the stately trees, searching for the elusive grouse that concentrated there because of the abundant beechnuts. I transmelded my thoughts with his, hinting at a curious blow down, and he subconsciously altered his path toward the fallen black cherry tree. As he approached, his ever-roaming eyes were drawn to the upright form of a strange stone.

Canaan Valley is literally covered with tens of thousands of stones of various sizes, but most lie flat. Brushing away ferns, leaves, and a small branch, the hunter read the inscription and was riveted by the date of 1880. A writer as well as a hunter, he had published a few articles about the history of Canaan Valley and knew of no man-made object bearing a date as old as 1880.

His curiosity piqued, I was confident the hunter would investigate further and, ultimately, I hoped, document the presence of my gravestone and describe the history of the Leatherman clan in Canaan Valley. And more importantly, I foresaw that he would preserve the details of my life, thus revealing me, G.S.L., to have been a real-life individual who lived—and died—in Canaan Valley.

CHAPTER TWO

The George W. Leatherman Family

My father, George W. Leatherman, was born on the family farm along Patterson Creek in Hampshire County, Virginia in 1835. In 1857, he married Mary S. Whip, my mother-to-be. My oldest brother, Warner, was born in 1859 and one year later my father was drafted into the Hampshire Guards, one of thirteen companies of Confederate soldiers organized in Hampshire County. He served less than one year and decided he did not want to fight for the rebels.

A cousin, Benjamin Leatherman, had moved his family to Indiana five years earlier and sent several letters describing the rich farmland that rewarded those persons venturesome enough to cross the Appalachian Mountains. After many agonizing family meetings around the crude kitchen table my father reluctantly reached the decision to leave Virginia.

By the dark of night Dad left Virginia, pushing his brown stallion until they reached the Ohio River. Relatives transported Mary and one-year old Warner to Romney where they boarded the steam-powered Baltimore and Ohio train. From there they rode through the mountains to Terra Alta, Fairmont, and Mannington, eventually reaching Wheeling and the Ohio River. After crossing the river they boarded the Central Ohio Railroad to Indiana. My father said many times that if it had not been for the railroads they never would have undertaken the trip to Indiana. Travel by horseback would have been too slow and arduous for the young family.

My second oldest brother, John, was born in Indiana in early 1862, and later that year the George W. Leatherman family returned to Hampshire County. I remember my father talking about their brief sojourn to Indiana, and how my mother missed her family back in Virginia. But I know no additional details of that small but significant chapter in my family's life.

Although the War Between the States had escalated by 1862, there was no pressure for my father to rejoin the Confederate forces. Locals, the majority of whom supported the Confederate cause, recognized his neutrality and religious leanings, and our farm suffered no major damage from the thousands of troops that moved through the South Branch Valley (South Branch of the Potomac River).

Confederate troops did take all his horses and beef cattle, but let him keep the milk cows. Dad often told us how the family had a big garden plus plenty of milk, cheese, and butter. With no horses available, plowing, hoeing, and hay harvest were done by hand. Most summer days Dad worked from daylight to dark swinging a scythe and a pitchfork, pressing relentlessly to store enough hay to allow his milk cows to survive the long winters.

The farm was close enough to Romney that both Confederate and Union troops were regular visitors. The Virginia military, under the Southern Confederacy, controlled Romney at the beginning of the war. However, on June 11, 1861, locals received their first view of blue-coated Union soldiers. General Lew Wallace informed the Romney citizens they would be perfectly secure, and no unarmed person would be harmed. Despite this announcement, most persons living in and around Romney fled to Harpers Ferry where Confederate troops were in command.

Dad explained to us that Romney was considered strategic to winning the war because of the significance of the Baltimore and Ohio Railroad in transporting troops and supplies. Although no major battles were fought in or around Romney the town changed hands fifty-six times—three times in one day alone.

Mom told about Stonewall Jackson, the famed Union general, stopping with his troops at the Leatherman cabin and asking permission to water their horses one day when Dad was out working. She said he was an imposing, powerful looking man, but treated her kindly. Dad confirmed Jackson's presence in the area, detailing that his troops took possession of Romney in January 1862 and held it for two months.

A third son, Zedekiah, was born in 1867, and a daughter, Mary Elizabeth, joined the family in 1869. Two years later, May 6, 1871, I entered this world. Although born in the same log cabin as our oldest brother, I was officially born in Mineral County, which had split off from Hampshire County in 1866. Of no less significance, I was officially born in West Virginia, not Virginia; that portion of Virginia west of the Alleghenies recognized as a separate state by President Abraham Lincoln in 1863.

Spirit entity and human entity joined a few hours after my birth. I have no recollection of the sudden shock of bright light and cold temperatures that accompanied my emergence, but I remember being bathed in warm water and wrapped in a freshly boiled cloth.

Four years later, in 1875, my brother, Daniel, was born. My mother was sick during the latter part of her difficult pregnancy, and the doctor from Romney never could relieve her pain. She was in bed almost constantly during the last two weeks before Daniel was born. Caroline Thrush, a family friend, and Sarah Leatherman, one of my aunts who was an experienced midwife, lived with us for the entire two weeks.

Late one afternoon my mother's cries of pain became so alarming that Dad told us kids to gather our wool blankets and plan to sleep in the barn that night. He built a small fire in front of the large, double barn doors and we grilled a nice fat raccoon over the flames while large potatoes roasted beneath a pile of hot coals. Warner and John had shot the coon the previous night when it was treed by our hound, Ulysses.

While sitting around the fire, Warner and John told hunting tales while Dad told about his grandparent's trip over the Atlantic from Germany. I fell asleep in Dad's arms, but jerked awake when Mom let out a loud, piercing scream. Sometime around midnight, with the Big Dipper high overhead, we retreated to our sweet-smelling beds in the hay.

None of us slept much, and, based on her screams, my Mother didn't sleep at all. As the first faint promise of daylight seeped through the wide cracks of the barn, my Mother's cries brought us upright from our blankets. Then all was quiet. Not too long after, my aunt Sarah came to the barn and announced that we had a new baby brother.

Following the birth of Daniel, my Mother's cries of pain halted—for a few hours. However, the log cabin where we lived was not a quiet place. Brother Daniel cried more than I liked, although admittedly I had never lived in a house with a baby. Most alarming to us children were the small, sharp gasps of pain and the near-constant whimpering of my Mother. Aunt Sarah, who had assisted with nearly 100 births, said Mom had childbed fever. She kept wet towels on her head, but the fever never subsided.

By the second day after Daniel's birth, Dad sent Warner into Romney to get Dr. Snyder, who arrived riding a small black mare, with his medical satchel strapped behind the saddle. Once again, we were sent to the barn to sleep. The Doctor cut small slits in mother's wrists, and bled her several times the first night, hoping to rid her of the life-threatening fever. He said she suffered from erysipelas, a serious infection. We were allowed to visit Mom the next day, but could only stay a few minutes at a time. She was so weak and pale that I became frightened and began to cry.

The doctor stayed that night, during which time he dosed Mom with powdered echinacea and quinine to stop the infection. Dad gave him a chicken and a slab of dried beef in payment for his services. We heard him tell Dad as he prepared to mount his mare, "I'm sorry but there's nothing more I can do."

I didn't know what that meant.

As we sat on the front porch the following day we could hear Dad talking to Mom. She was so frail that she could not sit up, but her voice remained firm. "George W.," she said, "You must make me a promise." She called me Little George, to distinguish me from my Dad. "Do you remember when your cousin's wife died and they put a wooden cross and a wooden board with her name carved in it on her grave? Then your cousin and the rest of the family moved to Indiana? Now, not even ten years later, the cross and the board have fallen over and are nearly rotted away. In a few years there'll be no sign of her grave. I'm dying, and you must promise me something." At these words my six-year-old sister Elizabeth gasped and began sobbing uncontrollably.

Dad started to say something but Mom interrupted. "Promise me you'll put a real stone on my grave. And one more thing, promise me you'll put a real stone with carved names on the gravestones of any of our children who die before you do."

Dad said instinctively, "You're not dying. The doctor said you just need some rest."

Obviously agitated, Mom forcibly repeated, "Promise me you'll do it!"

"I promise," Dad answered. "I'll put a real stone on your grave and one on each of our children's graves—if I'm still alive. But we aren't going to need theirs or yours for several years."

In a voice so low we could barely hear the words, Mom murmured, "I'm tired, so very tired, and my body aches all over. I can't hold my eyes open. Kiss me to seal your promise and leave me alone while I go to sleep."

She did go to sleep, but she never woke up. As the sun eased above Mill Creek Mountain the next morning, Dad entered the barn and solemnly announced, "Your mother died during the night. She's gone home to the Lord."

Elizabeth and I began crying, while our older brothers said nothing. We buried Mom two days later in a crude, pine coffin that Warner and John built. Neighbors and relatives had dug the grave and brought food. I vividly remember the hymns they sang that night while crowded in the cabin and the front porch: "I Love To Tell The Story," "Tell Me The Old, Old Story," and "What A Friend We Have In Jesus."

At the burial, Dad and each of us Leatherman children threw a shovel of dirt onto the coffin. After we returned to the cabin our neighbors finished filling the grave. Little did anyone know, or suspect, I would be the next of the Leatherman family to be lowered into the ground.

Mom had produced enough milk for Daniel during the first two days of his life, but by the third day her supply was inadequate. My aunt Sarah was about to wean her own son, and said she had enough milk for Daniel. Her family had a herd of Jersey cows and they always had plenty of milk in the house. Dad didn't have a choice. He figured he was going to have enough trouble keeping us five kids fed and healthy. During the next year, we saw Daniel only the five or six times when we made weekend visits.

My older sister, Elizabeth, became my substitute mother. Although only two years older, she was mature enough to prepare my meals, mend my clothes, and keep me out of serious trouble.

CHAPTER THREE

The New Housekeeper

Dad had asked Caroline Thrush, the woman who helped care for Mom during Daniel's birth, to stop by three days a week and prepare meals and wash dirty clothes. Caroline had never married and appeared to be the type of woman who would rather be known as a good cook than a good looker. She was tall and skinny, with black eyes and long, dark black hair that reached the middle of her back. She had been betrothed to a young man who lived in Romney, but he was killed in the battle of Gettysburg. For nearly ten years she had deeply grieved his loss, during which time she lived with her parents, Richard and Francis. Although there were several unmarried men in Hampshire County, Caroline discouraged them all when they showed any interest in courting.

Dad originally hired Caroline to come to the house three days each week, but her weekly stay extended to four days, and then to five by the end of two months. My Dad and older brothers were pleased to have her around the cabin, because there was always a hot supper ready when they returned after a long day cutting timber.

Dad had been hired to supply logs to the local sawmill. The timbers produced at the sawmill were used by the Baltimore and Ohio Railroad to rebuild bridges that had been destroyed during the Civil War.

My sister, Elizabeth, and I did not especially like Caroline. She was mean to us, scolding us for whining or spilling things, and almost every day she smacked us with a hickory switch. She was careful not to switch us on the bare legs where a red welt would show, and was usually nice to us after Dad came home each evening. We complained to Dad, but he said we should behave and Caroline would be nice to us.

Caroline was much meaner to Elizabeth than to me. My sister said it was because Caroline had always longed for a daughter of her own. If Caroline's betrothed had not died in the Civil War she might have had a daughter about the same age as Elizabeth. My sister thought Caroline needed a family.

My sister and I were the best of friends. We were always able to feed ourselves, watch for rattlesnakes and copperheads, and do most of the chores Dad assigned us. Sometimes we got into a little trouble, but usually nothing serious. Elizabeth was seven years old and I was five. I don't remember many details about the year Mom died, but Elizabeth reminded me of several little incidents when I was older.

Caroline would send us out to gather apples and tell us to not come home until our baskets were full. When she could think of nothing else for us to do she sent us to the garden to pull weeds. We decided she did not want us in the house. When we returned to the cabin and announced that we were done, she usually marched us right back out and walked between every row searching for even the smallest weed. For every one she found we received a smack with the hickory switch. She warned us not to tell our Dad or she would quit coming to the house to help. We knew there was no other person who would help and Dad and my brothers would be disappointed if she left. Lizzie, as I called my sister, said I should be tough and she would think of something to do to get back at Caroline.

Lizzie and I liked to catch small animals and bring them home. Sometimes we kept them in baskets or buckets to show our brothers when they returned from work. Zedekiah was only four years older than I, and he seemed impressed whenever we showed him some unusual frog or snake we had captured.

Caroline was afraid of snakes, including the ones that were so small they couldn't hurt a baby. She didn't even like the cute salamanders we brought to the house. She would tolerate the bright orange ones with red spots that crawled slowly across the yard, but she definitely did not like the big slimy ones that we found under rocks.

Caroline enjoyed making us gather eggs from the henhouse, even though she knew we didn't like the chore. Dad, Warner, and John had built a neat row of little open-fronted boxes inside the henhouse where the hens could lay their eggs. Each cubicle, which was lined with hay, was large enough for a hen to sit in without being cramped. Daily, each of our laying hens would go into the henhouse and jump up into one of the little boxes. When done laying an egg, each hen would cackle a few times, jump down from the box, and return to the yard or garden to hunt bugs.

The henhouse was dark and musty, having only two small windows. Typically, the hens laid their eggs at the back of a nesting box, forcing Lizzie and me to reach far into each box and feel for eggs. Sometimes an old, dark-feathered hen was sitting in the rear of the box and we would not see her. She would usually give us a good hard peck on the hand when we reached in. We would jump, yell, and sometimes even cry. A sharp peck would raise a welt and even bring some blood.

Unfortunately, people are not the only ones that like to eat chicken eggs. Sometimes, late at night, we would hear squawking in the henhouse and know a predator was trying to catch a hen or eat some eggs. Ulysses would begin barking, Dad and my brothers would start yelling, and the grand commotion brought everyone out of the house.

Lizzie and I sort of enjoyed the ruckus, although we knew that the presence of predators meant fewer eggs in the skillet. Raccoons, foxes, and weasels were the main culprits. Our hound Ulysses slept on the porch and would usually hear or smell raccoons or foxes before they got into the henhouse. However, weasels were much smaller, and did not seem to give off much odor. Ulysses seldom detected them.

Invasion of the henhouse by a weasel was typically not discovered until the next day when we went to gather eggs. The headless body of one of our dark-feathered hens sprawled on the floor beneath the roosting poles was evidence that a stealthy weasel had been successful in its nocturnal hunt. Almost always, if there was one dead hen there was usually a second. A hungry weasel apparently needed two hens to satisfy its blood lust. The death of a hen was a serious loss, but Lizzie and I were not totally distraught upon making the gruesome discovery. Fried chicken was one of our favorite foods.

If Caroline was at our house when a chicken died she would build a wood fire under the big black kettle we kept behind the smokehouse.

When the water began to boil, she repeatedly dipped the hen into the water until she could pluck handfuls of soggy feathers from the headless bird. The process was no different than when we caught a live hen and cut off its head with a hatchet.

After all feathers were removed and the yellowish skin glistened, the innards were removed. The hen would be hung in the springhouse, suspended over the cooling milk cans for the rest of the day. Old hens, too tough to fry, were cut up into pieces and dropped into simmering water on the cook stove. There they stewed until tender.

The liver, heart, gizzard, and egg sack were always set aside for cooking, along with the feet. While the organs were nutritious and tasty, the feet were nothing more than an oddity. Lizzie and I would drop the feet into boiling water and watch carefully until they turned a bright golden yellow. After they cooled we scraped the inedible scales off the lower legs then chewed off the fleshy pads on the underside of the toes and the stringy tendons that connected to each toe. Although there was no meat on the feet, chewing each slimy bone was great, messy fun.

Large black snakes liked chicken eggs as much as did my family, and apparently were able to smell the eggs some distance away. The alarmed hens would usually announce when one was around during the daytime, but at night a snake could slither silently into the henhouse. Black snakes were excellent climbers, and had no trouble climbing into the henhouse and then up into the laying boxes.

A black snake in a laying box did not like a hand groping around near it anymore than did a cranky old hen. We would usually bang on the side of each nest box, hoping to force a marauding black snake to exit, or at least vibrate its tail and announce its presence. On each henhouse visit, I could imagine a huge black snake, eyes unblinking, tail vibrating rapidly, head held erect ready to strike, muscles pulsating along its ribs, and sides slowly contracting and expanding.

Several times Lizzie and I accidentally grasped a black snake while feeling for eggs. We usually had time to jump back before the snake bit us, especially if it had swallowed two or three eggs. Other times the snake would strike and bring even louder screams of pain and surprise than did an irritated hen. Black snakes are not poisonous, but they certainly have sharp teeth.

We really weren't afraid of the black snakes, even those six feet long, but didn't like to be surprised by them. We kept a cane with a hooked handle leaning in one corner of the henhouse. When we found a blacksnake we would hook it with the end of the cane and gently pull it out of the box. We would then carry it to the barn where we hoped it would eat mice. Our five cats did a good job of reducing rodents around our farm buildings, but didn't have the climbing ability or patience of a blacksnake.

One day when hoeing our patch of sweet corn, Lizzie and I found a small puffing adder, about one foot long. These snakes typically rear up and spread their necks, trying to look like a dangerous venomous serpent, thus the basis for the name. In reality they aren't poisonous, and generally won't even bite a person if picked up.

When disturbed, they commonly roll over on their backs with their mouths wide open and pretend to be dead. If rolled onto their bellies, they immediately roll onto their backs. Lizzie and I had caught and played with dozens of them. They also have upturned noses that cause some people to call them hog-nosed snakes.

As we were playing with this snake, Lizzie had a delightful idea. She said, "Little George, we'll put this adder in the basket when we collect eggs this afternoon and take it to Caroline. When she takes out the eggs she'll find the snake and get all scared. We might get a switching, but it'll be worth it to see her scream and yell and jump all over the kitchen. She'll be as mad as a wet hen. She might be so frightened that she'll leave and never come back."

I thought it was a tremendous idea, and figured that the switching we would receive wouldn't hurt all that much. We hid the snake in our lunch basket, and talked and giggled all afternoon, in anticipation.

In the henhouse later that afternoon we put the snake on the bottom of the basket and carefully piled eggs on top. Working hard to keep the grins off our faces, we anxiously carried the heaped basket inside. Caroline was in the kitchen and didn't say a word when Lizzie handed her the basket. We immediately headed for the front porch.

Caroline usually sorted through the eggs, selecting cracked ones to cook for supper. The others were carried to the springhouse where they would be kept cool until needed. At the first scream, we glanced inside and spotted two broken eggs on the floor, the puffing adder squirming in the middle of the kitchen table, and Caroline scrambling for the back door. We jumped off the porch and ran for the barn. We solemnly agreed to say the snake must have crawled into the basket when we set it down outside the chicken house.

Supper was unusually quiet that evening. Caroline had left for her own house shortly after Dad and our brothers returned from logging. She left a big pot of beef stew on the stovetop and set the biscuits in the warming oven before leaving.

We sheepishly entered the cabin and took our seats at the long, wooden-plank table. Dad sat in a large chair at one end while Warner sat at the other end, the spot formerly occupied by our Mother. John and Zedekiah sat on a long bench on one side and Lizzie and I sat on a somewhat taller bench on the other. After the long, detailed blessing, Dad served himself and began passing the biscuits and butter around the table.

Not a word was said until Dad finished his first bowl of stew along with two biscuits. Solemnly pushing back his chair, he looked directly at Lizzie and me and said, "Caroline told me she had a horrible fright today and wouldn't be coming back tomorrow. She said there was a big poisonous snake in the egg basket and she narrowly escaped being bitten."

I immediately proclaimed, "It was only a harmless little ole puff adder."

Lizzie glared at me and said nothing. I had forgotten about our solemn promise. Our three brothers tried to keep straight faces, but Zedekiah burst out laughing.

I thought I detected a slight grin on Dad's face, but couldn't be sure. It disappeared as quickly as it came, and I knew Lizzie and I were in trouble. Dad sternly ordered, "Mary Elizabeth, go get the hickory switch that's hanging by the fireplace." He used a hickory switch when we committed small mischievous acts, but the leather belt when we were guilty of serious sins. He ordered Lizzie to bend over his chair, and asked, "Do you want three whacks or two?"

Between clinched jaws, she mumbled, "I guess two will be enough."

When it was my turn I remembered what Lizzie had told me, "Yell as loud as you can when he gives you the first whack and he'll ease up on the second one." Dad asked if I wanted three whacks or two and ordered me to bend over his chair.

Even before the switch struck my behind I began yelling, "Stop, stop! It hurts something awful!" Sure enough, the second whack wasn't even half as hard as the first. Regardless, I continued yelling as if in terrible pain.

Dad sent both of us upstairs to our bedroom and told us we must apologize to Caroline—if she ever returned.

Caroline did not come back the next week or the next and it didn't take long for us to miss her cooking. Lizzie and I tried to have a satisfying meal ready when Dad and our brothers came home from work, but we didn't have much imagination or cooking skills. Mom had taught Lizzie lots of things about cooking, but not enough for her to handle the entire task on her own.

For breakfast we had fried eggs and a cup of milk. Every afternoon we would conscientiously build a fire in the cook stove, set a big stew pot on top, and fill it with potatoes, onions, and chunks of dried beef. By the end of the first week even Lizzie was getting tired of the same old food. By the end of the second week it was obvious we needed Caroline to prepare our meals. Lizzie and I agreed that we could tolerate her meanness in return for her cooking.

CHAPTER FOUR

Wedding Announcement

Lizzie and I eventually learned to tolerate Caroline, although she continued to punish us for small, insignificant mischievous acts. With no warning, Dad announced at supper one night that he was going to marry Caroline. Warner, John, and Zedekiah were not surprised. Lizzie and I were stunned, and said nothing. I think we missed our Mother more than anyone else in the family—even Dad.

Lizzie, being the only girl, was my mother's favorite and the two of them had shared many chores, conversations, and secrets. Although I was the youngest, Mom had raised three other boys and it seemed I was nothing special to her. But she was the only Mother I had, and she had taken good care of me. She read to me almost every day, and taught me most of my letters. I could even write my own name.

While hunting ramps three days after Dad's surprise announcement, Lizzie and I had a long, serious talk. She said, "Little Georgie, I've given this matter much thought and concluded I don't want a new mother. If I can't have my real mother then I don't want any. I've decided to leave home. You're the only friend I have in the whole world and I want you to run away with me."

I answered, "You're my best friend, Lizzie, and I'll go where ever you go. One thing worries me though. I'm only five years old, and my short legs won't allow me to walk very far before I get tired."

Lizzie responded, "I've been thinking on this for the last couple nights and concluded that you'll need to ride. Dad depends on the horses to haul logs and plow the fields, so we can't take one of those. The only solution is for you to ride a cow. Since you and I drink more milk than anyone else they can certainly spare one of the cows. We'll take Belle, the young Jersey that just started giving milk. I raised her from a calf and she'll follow me like a puppy dog."

With much trepidation, I answered, "But Lizzie, I never rode a cow in my life and never heard of anyone who did. That three-year-old is a little frisky and probably won't like me sitting on her back."

Lizzie always had lots of confidence and said, "Don't worry, we'll start training her tomorrow. She's really smart and can learn quickly. Remember how I taught her to carry two baskets thrown over her back? After Dad and the boys leave for work we'll bring her back into the barn, give her a little corn to eat, and then gently lay a sack of corn across her back. She'll soon learn to associate the weight on her back with a reward."

Training began the next morning. We told Caroline we were going to play in the barn and she seemed glad to get us out of the house. Belle was grazing with the other three milk cows. Lizzie walked right up to her, fed her a handful of corn, and slipped a rope around her neck. Belle didn't want to leave the other cows but obediently followed Lizzie—and the corn she held—back to the barn. We entered the back door so Caroline would not see what was taking place.

We first placed the two baskets over Belle's back and added weight to each one. After lifting the baskets on and off several times we replaced them with a burlap sack half filled with corn. Lizzie fed the cow shelled corn while I walked around and leaned on her side. When Warner and John milked her they always leaned their head against her side while pulling on the teats. After an hour of training we removed the sack of corn and took Belle back to the pasture.

After five days of clandestine training I climbed up on the three-legged milk stool and, with Lizzie's help, managed to get on Belle. She got fidgety but calmed down when Lizzie fed her a handful of shelled corn. I was quite nervous that first day and sat real still.

By the third day I was able to move around on Belle's back and climb on and off without her being bothered. One thing we learned was not to grab Belle's horns, even though they were excellent handholds. Every time that happened she jumped and kicked wildly.

By the second week, Lizzie was able to lead Belle while I rode on her back, grasping a rope tied around her neck. I fell off three times the first day. I landed on my shoulder the first time and almost cried, but Lizzie told me to be tough and rub it a whole bunch. My shoulder turned black and blue the next day, but no one saw it but Lizzie. I told her I was afraid I might land on my head and crack my skull if I should hit a big rock. She told me not to be such a big sissy. We continued our cow training in the woods where there were no big rocks and the layers of fallen leaves cushioned my falls.

With our cowmanship progressing nicely, we felt confident that our run-away trip would be a success. Lizzie could write many words, although her spelling was not too good. Mom had taught her enough so she was able to make a rough list of the things we would take. Two blankets, some corn for the cow, a bag of food for us, a small skillet, candles, a few extra clothes, and some matches were the main items. Lizzie was sure we could find plenty of water to drink, grass for the cow to eat, and fallen limbs for our fires.

With the wedding less than two weeks away, we began planning our departure. Lizzie wanted to leave right away, but I thought we should wait until after the wedding. She said, "Caroline will be happy we're gone and will enjoy her wedding even more knowing she won't find any snakes in the flower baskets."

I uttered my main concern, "Dad might be a little sad we are gone, and will worry about us during the wedding."

Lizzie said, "I'll write him a note telling him we've gone to stay with Grandma Essie up near Short Gap. I'll list all the things we're taking with us and he'll realize we won't be in any danger. Dad knows I've been taking care of you since Mom died and he'll not worry. Besides, he seems so excited about his wedding that he'll be glad to be shed of us."

Our 300-acre farm was located in the broad valley situated between Knobly Mountain and Mill Creek Mountain. Similar to most mountains in eastern West Virginia, these angled in a southwest to northeast direction. Lizzie planned for us to take the small road that followed Patterson Creek. This mid-sized stream flowed northeast towards the Potomac River. The road passed through a mix of forest and farm, with most farmhouses set back from the road several hundred yards. We would be visible from a few of the farmhouses if the people happened to be working outside.

Caroline was coming to our house four or five days a week, and Lizzie reckoned we would leave on one of the days Caroline was not at the house. We slowly accumulated the items on our list, and hid everything in the barn. Lizzie knew how to hard boil eggs and we planned to take at least twenty on our trip. She said we could secretly boil two or three each day and no one would ever know about it. She also planned to take several potatoes. We had several bushels of dried apples in the fruit cellar, and Lizzie assured me our family would want us to take a big sack full.

We made one last trip to visit Mom's grave and placed some fresh-dug Christmas ferns near her wooden marker. We usually visited the grave at least once each week, cleaning off weeds, planting flowers, and straightening the cross and marker. At such times we would both tell her how we missed her and how Caroline was so mean to us. Lizzie and I would usually start crying. We would hug each other and remind ourselves that at least we had each other.

CHAPTER FIVE

Run-Aways

The wedding was planned for a Saturday, and Lizzie and I left the previous Tuesday. As soon as Dad and our brothers left for work, Lizzie caught the cow while I readied the baskets with all our food and belongings. We quickly loaded Belle and started down the road to Short Gap.

Lizzie wore a flowery, feed sack dress, which almost reached her ankles, and I wore a white shirt and a pair of gray pants with straps over my shoulders to hold them up. We both wore heavy leather shoes and a wool coat. As we set off on our great adventure, I fingered the asafetida bag my Mom had made to ward off evil spirits and keep me healthy. Mom had been confident the asafetida would prevent chest colds. Approximately the size of my thumb, the soft leather bag was suspended by a leather thong hung around my neck. Its primary contents were a vile-smelling resin from fennel roots, plus ground goldenseal and echinacea. Mom had painted a small daisy on the bottom of the bag, and I was reminded of her every time I looked at the flower. Most youngsters my age wore an asafetida bag, but by the time they were teen-agers they rebelled against its disgusting odor.

I walked awhile but soon grew tired and Lizzie led Belle alongside a small boulder so I could climb aboard. We were in a gay mood, shed of Caroline and on our own.

Lizzie started singing, "Yankee Doodle went to town, riding on pony. Put a feather in his hat and called it macaroni." Then she quickly revised it and continued, "Georgie Leatherman went to town, riding on a heifer. Put a flower in his cap and called it apple butter."

I laughed so hard that I grabbed Belle's horns to keep from falling. That frightened the cow and when she gave a wild jump I toppled into the roadside ditch. Lizzie managed to hold onto Belle's rope while I slowly pulled myself out of the mud. I banged my head on a small rock and felt woozy when I stood up. After Lizzie tied Belle to a small tree we sat on the roadside for a while until I began to feel better. Lizzie offered me some dried apples and in a short time I was ready to resume our trip.

By mid-morning my legs were so tired I could go no further. The sun was shining brightly and temperatures had climbed so high we removed our coats. It was a beautiful spring day. We stopped for a rest and had a hard-boiled egg and a few handfuls of dried apples.

Belle found a thick patch of grass to eat and Lizzie and I took a little nap. I woke refreshed and we continued our journey. Around mid-day we spotted a small stream not far from the road and stopped to eat again. We ate two more eggs, some bread, and more dried apples. After playing in the creek we took a nap, sleeping almost one hour. Belle was resting under a big tulip poplar while she contently chewed her cud and Lizzie said we should let her continue. She explained that cows could not chew their cud while walking.

I told her, "I'm really lucky to have such a smart sister."

As the sun was setting, we passed a hay barn sitting on a small knoll in the middle of a pasture. No houses or other buildings were in sight. The barn was half-filled with hay, apparently left over from the previous summer. Lizzie decided the owner wouldn't mind if we spent the night so we opened the big double doors, unloaded Belle, and carried all our belongings inside.

Tying the cow to the side of the barn, we gathered our small tin pail and took turns milking her. Lizzie had milked on several occasions and knew exactly what to do; squeeze and pull, squeeze and pull, squeeze and pull. Then grab the two other teats and repeat the process. She managed to half fill the pail, and said it was my turn. I tried really hard, but my small hands weren't strong enough to coax a stream of milk. I managed to produce a few squirts but soon gave up. Lizzie tried again and eventually managed to nearly fill the small pail. We had counted on milk for breakfast and supper, and could see that this demanding chore might be more than we could handle.

After fastening a leather hobble around Belle's two right legs we turned her loose to graze. Downed tree limbs were plentiful in the nearby woods and we soon had a large pile of wood ready for an evening fire. The weather was unseasonably mild, however, and we didn't actually need a fire to keep warm or cook our food.

After a supper of bread, eggs, dried beef, and milk we leaned against the side of the barn and Lizzie started singing, "Georgie Leatherman went to town, riding on a cow. Stuck a splinter in his toe and called out, ow ow ow."

Our self-assurance began to lag at dark and the eerie call of a screech owl crept out of the woods. I said, "Don't you think we should light the fire, I'm getting a little cold." I really wasn't, but I didn't want to sit there in the dark and listen to all the scary night sounds.

Using only one match, Lizzie soon had the kindling burning and before long the soft flames reassured and comforted us. We had stacked the branches ten feet from the barn and scraped all hay away from the area to prevent our fire from escaping. Worn out from the day's adventure, I soon dozed off.

As the last of our firewood was reduced to glowing red coals Lizzie shook me awake and said we should go to bed. We had spread our blankets on the hay inside the barn earlier that evening and were soon nestled close together. A whip-poor-will started its monotonous serenade and continued nearly nonstop for what seemed like an hour, as was their usual custom. It frightened me a little, and I suggested, "Maybe we should shut the barn door so Belle doesn't wander inside during the night and eat a bunch of the farmer's hay. And, it probably wouldn't hurt to bar the door so Belle doesn't push it open."

Lizzie answered, "That's not a bad idea, Little Georgie. It's too late to shut the barn door after the horse gets out. Or in this case, after the cow gets in." She scrambled out of bed, closed the door, and hurried back to her blanket.

I slept fitfully, but woke well rested. Belle had not wandered far and our first chore was to bring her to the barn where we would attempt to milk her. Lizzie started, but soon complained that her hands ached. I tried, but again was unsuccessful. I gained more respect for the ease with which Dad, Warner, and John could quickly fill a large pail. Lizzie finally managed to half fill the small pail but it required nearly one hour for her to do so.

After breakfast we loaded the milk pail, with its tight-fitting lid, into one of the baskets and resumed our journey. We were well rested and made much better time down the dusty road than we had the first day. Within the hour, we sighted a lone rider on a handsome black horse coming toward us. We soon identified the rider as a man we had seen in church. Lizzie thought his name was Cosner.

The man brought his black horse to a stop and studied us carefully. We must have made an interesting pair: Lizzie slightly chubby, with short, curly blonde hair, and blue eyes much like those of our mother, and me with sun-bleached, reddish-blonde hair, a few freckles, and dark brown eyes. With a friendly greeting, the rider asked, "Where are you young'uns headed?"

Lizzie had already settled on the answer we would give if asked such a question and immediately answered, "Dad asked us to take this heifer to our grandmother up near Short Gap. Her old cow fell in the river and drowned. Our older brothers can't go because they're busy logging."

Cosner said nothing for several minutes as he continued to study the cow and the baskets she carried. He dropped the reins on his horse, slowly dismounted, and walked around Belle. Then he commented, "It looks like you didn't milk the cow completely dry this morning. Do you want me to finish the job?"

Lizzie hesitated, then answered, "We'd be obliged if you'd fill our pail so we can have plenty to drink with our lunch."

After I dismounted, Cosner knelt beside Belle, and in less than five minutes had filled the pail. He commented, "That should last until you can milk her this evening. Do you think you'll arrive at your grandmother's house tonight?"

Lizzie answered, "We figure it'll take us four or possibly five more days to reach her house, but we're in no hurry and have plenty of food."

Cosner mounted his horse, wished us luck on our journey, and continued up the dusty road. Lizzie and I decided to eat a snack at that spot, since we had a full pail of milk. Hard-boiled eggs, bread, and milk satisfied our appetite, and we were soon napping in the soft grass.

Upon wakening, I told Lizzie, "Someday I'll have my own horse and I'll be the best hunter in the area. I'll gallop down dusty roads, through heavy woods, across rocky creeks, and up steep mountainsides. Remember that picture of Buffalo Bill Cody we saw in that old newspaper in Romney? I might get me a big floppy hat like he wore and people will call me 'Cowboy George' when I ride into town."

Lizzie smiled a sisterly smile and answered, "I think you'll make a handsome cowboy, and I'll be proud to ride by your side. However, they might call you 'Jersey George' if they heard you had ridden a Jersey cow."

The warm, spring day progressed nicely, although we did not cover many miles. Stopping to eat a couple snacks, take a nap, catch a puffing adder, and turn over rocks in a small creek in search of crawdads slowed us down.

As dusk approached we searched in vain for another barn where we could spend the night. Lizzie thought it would be better if we spent the night in the woods rather than in an open field. I was not convinced, mindful of all the critters that lived in forests. We finally settled for a relatively open, flat spot in dense woods under a large, white oak tree.

Trying to calm my fears, Lizzie argued, "We have plenty of sticks and branches, and can keep a fire burning all night."

With the two baskets removed from Belle and our blankets spread over a deep pile of leaves, we began milking again. Lizzie did a little better than she had the previous morning, but I was of no help. With the cow tied to a small maple sapling, Lizzie milked awhile, ate awhile, milked awhile, and then ate some more. She could only pull and squeeze for about ten minutes before her hands started to ache. With the pail nearly full Lizzie gave up, although there was some doubt whether Belle had been milked dry.

The thick branches created by the stand of oaks effectively blocked out much of the late afternoon sun, and the gloomy forest produced a feeling of foreboding. I urged Lizzie to light the fire. The fire brought a sense of comfort and security. However, with nightfall came the fascinating night sounds—a nearby screech owl, a great horned owl in the distance, rustlings in the leaves, and various unidentified chirps and squeaks. My concerns were eased by the flames of our campfire, but the dancing shadows they created fueled my imagination. Movement was everywhere, and I finally had to force myself to not look at the surrounding trees. By gazing directly into the flames and studying the constantly changing colors and shapes I relaxed a bit.

As we made final preparations for bed, we threw several large limbs on the fire. At first I laid on my back, looking straight upward. However, the flickering shadows on the underside of limbs and leaves were too traumatic and I soon rolled over on my side facing the fire, as did Lizzie. We eventually fell asleep to the smells of burning wood, decomposing leaves, and rich earthy litter that covered the forest floor.

I have no idea how long we had been asleep, when Lizzie and I bolted upright. From somewhere out of the surrounding woods, a loud, piercing scream penetrated the darkness, followed quickly by two more. Tree limbs rustled violently and limbs slapped against trees, as if a small windstorm was advancing through the forest. Snarls and growls seemed to emanate from opposite sides of our small camp, causing Belle to emit a frightened bellow.

With a low, frightened voice, Lizzie said, "We need more limbs on the fire."

I quickly pulled the blanket over my head and answered, "I'm going to stay right here." Thank goodness I had such a brave sister, because in a short time the flames were visible through my blanket.

Lizzie and I snuggled close together, and I whispered, "What kind of animal made those sounds?"

"It sounded like a couple bears or possibly a wildcat fighting a bear," she answered.

I thought it must be a whole pack of bears or wildcats. One or two animals could not make that much racket. I had dozed slightly, mesmerized by the flickering flames, when the commotion resumed. This time it was closer, and seemed to come from a very angry animal.

In a low trembling voice, I mumbled, "I'm scared. I wish I were in a barn or in my own house." Lizzie reached over and held my hand, but said nothing.

Another long lull was followed by another scream. I almost started crying, but shoved the edge of the blanket in my mouth and closed my eyes. Several large sticks cracked nearby, as if something heavy had stepped on them. While I pulled the blanket even tighter over my head, Lizzie jumped up and yelled, "Get away from here! Get away, whatever you are!"

I was so frightened that I began to sing foolishly, "Yankee Doodle went to town, riding on a pony. Stuck a feather in his hat and called it macaroni...." I do not know how many times I repeated the verse before I started to cry.

The noises ceased shortly thereafter, and Lizzie left her blanket to throw the last of the wood on the fire. We figured the creature had either left or was waiting for the flames to die down before attacking. When nothing remained of the fire but glowing orange coals, Lizzie and I snuggled tightly against one another. But sleep would not come, and we were both awake when the pattering of rain on the leaves high overhead began.

At first, no drops penetrated the foliage, and the sounds were comforting. However, as the rainfall became heavier a few drops struck my blanket. Soon lightning flashed and thunder rumbled.

As the rain became heavier we were forced to take action. Lizzie said, "We're going to get soaked if this keeps up. It isn't cold, but we will be completely chilled if we sit here until daylight. We better move over to the base of the big oak. It's leaning slightly and will offer some protection."

The coals threw enough light that we could see the trunk of the giant white oak and in a few minutes the two of us were huddled together against the rough bark. We were comfortable enough at first, but eventually trickles of water ran down the trunk and were quickly sponged up by our blankets. When they became saturated we pulled them off and leaned our bodies away from the tree trunk. I reasoned that a soaked wool blanket was worse than being pelted by falling raindrops.

As a loud thunderclap shook the ground, I sobbed, "Lizzie, I'm not sure this trip was such a great idea. Do you think we could wait until we're a little older and try it again? I'm cold and wet and scared of that animal waiting to eat us."

Lizzie said, "Don't worry. When the sun comes up, we'll dry off and not have a thing to worry about."

When morning finally arrived, our clothes and blankets were soaked and we couldn't find any dry wood to start a fire. We ate a breakfast of soggy bread and hard-boiled eggs. Lizzie said, "Let's find Belle and get some nice fresh milk. That'll warm up your insides."

We began our search, but the cow was nowhere to be seen. We searched the area for almost an hour, but the soft litter of the forest floor was not conducive to tracking. Lizzie explained that the lightning and thunder had probably frightened Belle and she had run off. She said, "Do you remember how Dad used to tell us that horses could find their way home from long distances, whether in the dark, or rain, or snow? I bet that Belle is on her way home right now."

I replied, "We've got to find her. If she followed the road back towards our house then we better hurry and catch up with her. We'll be in a lot of trouble if we lose her."

We began our return trip with each one dragging a basket that Belle had carried. Because of the weight of the soaked wool blankets, we had to stop several times before finally coming to a pasture field. Fortunately for us the morning sun was shining brightly and we spread our blankets over some low shrubs. Within an hour our clothes had dried, but the blankets were still wet.

We started walking again, but I could not carry my share. I explained, "Lizzie, I can't drag a basket loaded with food and a soaked blanket. We're going to have to leave something behind."

"Alright, Little George. We'll leave our blankets and one of the baskets. Together, we should be able to carry enough food in one basket to get back home. We should be able to reach that barn by nightfall, and we can sleep in the hay tonight."

I liked the idea. That had been a nice barn. We could keep warm in a pile of hay and even bar the door if we wanted.

We searched the road as we walked, but saw no split-hoof tracks, only the single-hoof tracks of horses. Lizzie explained that Belle had probably not walked in the road, but in the adjacent meadow where she could graze. Lizzie always seemed to know what was going on.

It was nearly dark when the barn with double doors came into sight. My feet hurt terribly, but with renewed energy I managed to struggle inside. We ate a little, closed the barn doors, crawled into a pile of hay, and were soon asleep.

At the first faint light of day I awoke. Something was walking in the hay, coming ever closer. It was impossible to determine the size of the animal, but it made a distinct rustling as it crawled across the hay. It was too large to be a mouse, but too small to be a bear or bobcat. I wondered if the animal we heard in the woods the previous night had followed us to the barn. I reached over and squeezed Lizzie's arm. When the animal was approximately five feet away, Lizzie jumped up and began yelling, "Shoo! Get away! Get away from here!"

I felt something sting my eyes, and detected the overpowering odor that was impossible to mistake. Our visitor had been a skunk and both Lizzie and I had been sprayed. Fortunately, only a small amount entered my eyes, and the burning sensation soon stopped.

We were only faintly aware of the odor that penetrated the barn. Our sense of smell had been instantly numbed when the skunk struck. We knew from experience that the odor we carried would be much more obvious to other persons, even those ten to twenty feet away, than it was to us. After a hasty breakfast, we left the barn and continued our trek back up the road to our house.

As we struggled along the muddy road, I had terrible thoughts about the punishment that awaited us. We had lost the family's prize Jersey, our blankets, and one of the baskets. We smelled strongly of skunk. We would not be allowed to enter the house, let alone sleep in it. I asked Lizzie, "How many smacks do you think we'll get?"

She answered, "I'd guess it'll be at least ten, but it could be twenty. Remember, you must start yelling and screaming after four or five smacks, and maybe you'll get only ten."

As dusk settled over the South Branch Valley our log cabin finally came into view. No one was in sight, and we figured they must be in the house eating supper. I told Lizzie, "I'm scared. Why don't you go on and tell everyone that I got tired and will return sometime tomorrow."

"They'll never believe me," Lizzie said. "They know I would never leave you. We went away together and we'll return together."

CHAPTER SIX

Homecoming

Lizzie and I learned the following year that members of our family had been peering anxiously from cabin windows as we approached. When Dad and our brothers had returned home Tuesday evening, they became alarmed after reading Lizzie's note. They had reasoned it was too late to initiate a search that night and would wait until daylight. It was decided that George W. and Warren would return to the logging job, while John and Zedekiah went in pursuit of us kids.

At daylight the two boys started down the road riding their workhorses. Late that morning they met Cosner riding his high-stepping black. John asked, "Have you seen a young girl and a boy leading a Jersey cow?"

Cosner answered, "No, not exactly. But I did see a boy riding a cow with a girl walking beside. It was the dangest thing I ever saw. They appeared to be managing without too many problems, although they weren't able to milk the cow dry. Fortunately, the Jersey is young and isn't producing much milk. They were a short distance past the old Myers' barn and I expect you can catch up with them before dark."

Expressing their gratitude for his assistance, John and Zedekiah bid Cosner good-bye and urged their horses, Abe and Mack, down the road past the Myer's barn. The horses were named for two of Dad's heroes, President Abraham Lincoln and General George McClelland.

While their mounts plodded steadily through the dust the boys began making plans. Our family had decided Lizzie and I would run away again if forced to return home. John and Zedekiah needed to create a situation that would convince us to return on our own. Late that afternoon, as our two brothers topped a small hill they spotted us in the road nearly a quarter mile ahead.

When the three of us entered the dense woods, John reasoned we would be camping soon and most likely would build a fire. Our brothers waited until the sun dipped behind the hills before moving to the edge of the woods. After tying their horses to a tulip poplar sapling they started to approach us.

Their goal was to frighten Lizzie and me so badly we would call a halt to our trip and return home. The boys quietly stalked to within fifty yards of us. It was decided that Zedekiah would imitate the cries of a bobcat, while both boys banged long poles against tree trunks and branches. They would find the cow later and one of the boys would take her back to the Leatherman farm while the other kept a clandestine watch on us.

All went according to plan, and daylight found Zedekiah leading Belle back to our farm while John discretely followed us. John spent the night a short distance from the barn we slept in. When it was obvious Lizzie and I would arrive home safely that evening, John pushed his horse to a slow trot so he would reach the cabin first.

Dad had decided the family should act surprised when Lizzie and I entered the cabin. The roles of John and Zedekiah as noise makers would not be revealed and they would let Mary Elizabeth tell the story. However, all plans immediately changed when my sister and I walked through the cabin door.

As we neared the cabin, Liz had decided it would be best if she told the story of our trip. She would simply say we had changed our minds and thought Dad and Caroline would want the two us at their wedding. I agreed to keep quiet. However, before we had taken two steps inside the cabin we were startled by cries of, "Stop! Get back outside! Don't come in here!"

Skunk scent is very strange, being so permeating that it arrives before the person it adorns. During the twelve hours since our encounter with the skunk our sense of smell had become seriously impaired and we had forgotten about being sprayed. To Dad, Warren, John, and Zedekiah, however, the sudden wave of nauseating skunk scent was a shock.

Dad announced, "You two won't be sleeping in the cabin tonight. Go to the barn immediately and we'll bring your supper and a couple old horse blankets. I'm sure you won't mind camping out one more night. In the morning we'll give you a big bar of lye soap and you can try to scrub off that horrible smell. You can take your clothes to the creek and wash them at the same time."

As we lay on the smelly horse blankets, which had been repeatedly soaked with horse sweat, Lizzie reasoned that our skunk encounter was possibly a blessing in disguise. It appeared that we would not get a spanking—at least not that night.

We had another blessing too. Because the wedding was the next day, Dad decided we would not be welcomed at the church. We spent a couple hours vigorously scrubbing our clothes then decided to let our clothes dry in the mid-day sun.

Dad, Caroline, and our brothers returned late that afternoon. Although we did not directly observe their return, I could imagine Dad and Caroline riding together in the buggy. And I was not pleased with the image. We retreated to the barn when we heard the plopping of the horses' hooves on the dirt road and the jangling of harness. Zedekiah brought us our supper that evening, and informed us that we were to spend at least one more night in the barn, and possibly two. We really didn't mind, since we were in no hurry to welcome Caroline as a member of our family.

We never did get a spanking, possibly because Belle had rejoined the other cows, and Zedekiah retrieved the blankets and extra basket we had abandoned along the road. Lizzie and I talked about running away several times during the next couple months, but always postponed it for some reason. I told her I would go if we could stay in a barn every night, but I would not spend another night in the woods.

Lizzie and I gradually learned to tolerate Caroline, and she learned to tolerate us. She was too busy with Daniel and her other chores to worry about our minor mischief. Daniel was about nine months old and was eating mashed up people food along with Jersey cow milk. It took a while for us to get used to having a baby in the house but before long Lizzie was feeding him, teaching him to walk, and watching over him. By the time he was one year old, Lizzie was almost solely in charge of his care.

Every year on the anniversary of Mom's death, the entire family would visit her gravesite. We would remove all the fallen branches, plant new flowers, mow the grass, and Dad would say a few words. At our second anniversary visit, we found the wooden cross fallen over and the carved wooden board tilting precariously. In attempting to set both objects upright it became evident they were rotting at the base.

Lizzie firmly stated, "Dad, you promised Mom on her deathbed you would get her a stone grave marker, and you still haven't done it. She's probably turning over in her grave because of the sad condition of her cross and wooden marker. You better get it pretty soon or she'll start to haunt you."

Dad lowered his head and meekly answered, "I've been saving a little money each month and almost have enough. I'm planning to have one made next month."

CHAPTER SEVEN

The Fishing Trip

About a year after his marriage to Caroline, Dad started doing more things with his own family. Caroline would stay home taking care of Daniel while the rest of us went on outings. Especially memorable were those Saturdays when we loaded the wagon and ventured to pick blackberries or gather sweet chestnuts and juicy wild grapes. Dad would often say, "The land will feed you if you're willing to work. The lazy may go to bed hungry, but the hard-working will always have food on the table."

When I was seven years old, Lizzie and I were not able to spend much time together, because she was constantly taking care of Daniel. However, we did have a few long talks. I remember her telling me, "Caroline no longer seems to dream of her betrothed who died at Gettysburg, but longs to have a child of her own, one she can hold against her breast and take joy in knowing it is of her own creation. Maybe that's why she married Dad, certainly not to have a ready-made family."

Caroline did have a baby of her own when Daniel was two-years old. Emma, a tiny bit of a girl, joined our family. Lizzie, now nine years old, was given total responsibility for Daniel. I helped a little, but there wasn't much I could do. Thus, I spent several hours each day alone. I hunted frogs, snakes, and other critters in the small creek that ran past our house. I learned to identify many of the common birds, although I often did not know their correct name. When no one else knew the name I simply made one up.

Dad took my brothers and me on many fishing trips to Patterson Creek, bringing home dozens of large catfish, fallfish, and suckers that were dried in our smokehouse. The smoked filets were used to create soups and stews when fresh meat was not available, or when we just wanted a change of diet. They also provided a convenient snack that could be easily carried on outings.

When the weather turned nice in April we would set off for Patterson Creek in a wagon loaded with lanterns, extra food, blankets, baskets, wooden kegs, and long nets. As predictable as the return of Canada geese, the emergence of ramps, the blooming of serviceberry trees, and the sudden eruption of morel mushrooms, were the congregations of spawning suckers in tributaries of the South Branch River. When water temperatures reached forty degrees, suckers began their upstream migrations. White and hog suckers were abundant in high-gradient streams having stony riffles.

Although most spawning and upstream movements occurred at night, suckers were abundant enough during daylight hours to provide a rich harvest. At times the water would erupt with wildly fleeing suckers when we surprised a large congregation. Typically, my older brothers would spread nets across the streams, while the rest of us beat the water with long poles. Dozens of stunned, twenty-inch suckers drifted slowly downstream to be caught with dip nets or captured in the large nets spanning the creek. A good night yielded hundreds of the brilliantly colored white suckers.

Their backs were olive with a bright lavender sheen and the lateral band running lengthwise along the stream-lined bodies was a dazzling pink. All fish over ten inches in length were piled into baskets and wooden kegs. Later they were gutted and layered in salt for preservation.

As he did on other fishing trips, Dad repeated one of his favorite sayings, "As stated in an old Chinese proverb: Give a man a fish and you will feed him for a day. But teach a man to fish and you will feed him for a lifetime."

And as he had done on several occasions, Warner added, "Give a man a fish and you will feed him for a day. But teach a man to fish and he will never finish his chores."

John added, "Give a man a fish and you will feed him for a day. But teach a man to fish and he will be a liar for the rest of his life."

Not to be left out, Zedekiah added, "Give a man a fish and you will feed him for a day. But teach a man to fish and he will never have to eat possum."

One particular fishing trip was especially memorable. The overnight excursion was scheduled to depart Friday afternoon. As with other fishing trips, Warner and John hitched Abe and Mack to the wagon. Lizzie and I had earlier loaded the wagon with fishing poles, bait, crocks to hold the fish, food enough for all six of us, and blankets to keep us warm. We also threw in enough sweet-smelling hay to soften the bumpy ride down the rutted farm road and for sleeping later that night. When everyone had thrown in some extra clothes the adventure began.

Catfish and fallfish, which were so abundant in deep pools of the South Branch, were our main quarry. We arrived at the river at dusk, built several fires along the bank of the river, and prepared for the feeding forays of the large catfish. Smaller fish would be returned to the river, while eating-size ones would be safely secured to the riverbank by stringers until daylight arrived, when they would be cleaned for eating. The medium-sized fish would be fried for breakfast and lunch, while large ones would be filleted and placed in large earthen crocks. A layer of salt would preserve each layer of fish until we could get them to the smokehouse.

The older boys soon had three large fires roaring, providing plenty of light for us to safely move around, bait our hooks, and remove any fish we caught. Zedekiah caught the first fish, a channel cat almost two feet long. John caught a big fallfish then I caught a small catfish. We all started catching fish, with considerable bragging about how each was the largest so far.

There was no lack of excitement as the night progressed. Lizzie caught a hook in her thumb, but Dad expertly pulled it out without ripping too much flesh. He sucked the cut to remove any germs, spitting the blood on the ground at Lizzie's feet. With a small strip of clean cloth around her thumb, she continued fishing as if nothing had happened. Warner slipped off the bank into the river while trying to land a catfish almost three feet long, but the water was only waist deep, and we all laughed.

I accidentally stepped on a catfish that was flopping on the ground and ran its dorsal spine into the bottom of my foot. Dad jerked it out, sucked on it to remove the remaining poison, and rubbed some salt into the wound. I jumped and yelled and told him the salt hurt worse than the catfish spine. My older brothers were laughing uproariously, while Lizzie scolded them for being so inconsiderate towards their brother.

As the moon approached its zenith, I wandered away from the bright light of the fires, slightly upstream of the others, and settled into a nice soft bed of some type of leafy vegetation. The damp night air flowed over me leaving pleasant memories of the musty river mud, the bright, non-flickering evening star, the pungent, yet charming campfire smoke, and the bellowing bullfrogs. I awoke upon hearing Dad call my name. The fish had almost quit biting, so Dad decided we should try to get a little sleep before daylight returned. Zedekiah, Lizzie, and I slept in the bed of the wagon, while Dad and Warner slept underneath. John decided to continue fishing and to keep the fires burning.

John told us at breakfast that he heard three screech owls, four barred owls, numerous critters splashing in the river, plus some kind of big cat snarling and screaming. Lizzie and I both shivered as we remembered our ill-fated run-away adventure.

Warner and John cleaned enough small fish for breakfast, while Zedekiah built two cooking fires. Although it was May, the fires took the chill off the morning. Dad fried fish in one large black skillet at one fire, while Warner fried potatoes and eggs at the other. Before long, everyone had a tin plate piled high with fish, potatoes, and eggs. That trip was one of the fondest memories I retain of life in Mineral County.

The older boys and Dad filleted fish most of the morning while Lizzie and I hunted in the shallows for clams. After a lunch of more fried fish and potatoes, the horses were hitched to the wagon and we rolled down the road with crocks filled to the brim: eighty-five catfish fillets, thirty-six fallfish fillets, and twenty-three suckers.

Lizzie and I slept most of the way home. Following a supper of beef stew and cornbread, I went to bed with no coaxing. Upon my coming downstairs Sunday morning, Caroline asked, "Lord have mercy, child. Did you get in stinging nettle? Your face and arms are covered with red splotches!"

I answered, "No. I never felt any stinging at the river, but early this morning I did start to itch something fierce."

I went with the family to church, but by afternoon my entire face, neck, and most of my arms were covered with red splotches. I couldn't stop itching, although Dad warned me that would only make things worse. The welts became blisters the next day, and there was no doubt that I had gotten into poison ivy. I later figured that I must have lain in a thick bed of the toxic plant when I moved upstream of the fires and fell asleep.

I was well acquainted with poison ivy, learning young that I was super-susceptible to it. Dad quizzed me regularly when we were out in the fields, hoping that I would learn to recognize the shiny three-leaved plant without even trying. I had a few outbreaks before Mom died, but nothing too serious.

By Tuesday my eyes were swollen shut and I even had blisters on my tongue. By Wednesday, I was covered from head to toe. Blisters in my nostrils made breathing difficult. I was more miserable than at any other time in my life.

At Dad's suggestion, everyone in the family gathered jewelweed leaves until they had filled six large baskets. These were crushed and the bright green juice sprinkled over my blisters. A poultice of the crushed leaves was later plastered over the entire front of my body. Several hours later I turned over in bed and a fresh poultice was applied to the back of my body, legs, and arms.

Dad sent Warner to get Dr. Snyder in Romney, but there wasn't much he could do. He said they should change the bedding daily, because the fluids seeping from my blisters would cause further outbreaks. I don't know how they could have spread any more since there wasn't one inch of my body that was not already affected. After a few hours, the clean bedding was stained heavily with yellowish-brown splotches where my blisters had seeped.

I never did cry and Lizzie told everyone it was because I was tough.

Actually my nostrils and eyes were so swollen it wasn't possible to cry. Lizzie was the one who cried. On the fifth day, she broke down while reading to me, and sobbed, "It's all my fault! A sister is supposed to watch over her little brother. I can't stand seeing you in such misery. I'm not coming back to this bedroom until you start looking like a human being again."

Lizzie came back the next day, reciting poems and repeatedly cautioning me not to scratch. I couldn't help it. When awake I could tell myself to stop, but asleep I scratched places until they bled. That made my bedding even more disgusting. I lay naked in bed for five days until the condition started to subside.

By Saturday, two weeks after the fishing trip, my eyes were open and there were no blisters inside my mouth or nostrils. I could breathe properly and could finally eat solid food. Another week passed and I was able to walk without the intolerable itching. It was nearly a month before all symptoms completely disappeared.

In later years, I had a few more brushes with poison ivy, usually when accidentally encountered while digging for May apple roots in October or November. Fortunately, I never had another life-threatening outbreak. That overnight fishing outing was thereafter referred to as, Little George's Poison Ivy Trip.

CHAPTER EIGHT

Boyhood Adventures

By the time I was seven I would often spend entire days alone in the woods, often watching one individual animal for hours at a time. Of course, I first had to complete my chores; hauling in firewood, taking care of the garden, feeding the livestock, and gathering eggs. I discovered the den of a red fox on an east-facing hillside and watched from the cover of a fallen white pine as the parents brought rabbits and young groundhogs, and even a chicken to feed their young.

One late winter day I discovered the nest of a chicken hawk, as most people called them. This large hawk, with stunning reddish tail, frequently could be seen soaring high over our pastures. Dad said it was looking for chickens. I saw them catch several rabbits, but no chickens. The hawk's nest was lodged securely in the forks of a tulip poplar and was visible from the opposite hillside, at least until trees were fully leafed.

This was a very unusual pair: the female hawk was almost solid white, except for a few reddish-orange tail feathers, while the male was similar to all other chicken hawks I saw. His back was dark brown and his breast was speckled white. Dad explained that animals of white color were called albinos and were quite rare in the wild. In his entire life he had seen only four albino animals: a groundhog, a robin, a squirrel, and a partially white deer. I made a point to look at the nest over two years, but as far as I could tell all of the young were normal colored. I was disappointed not to see at least one white youngster.

By the time I was eight I had already raised several animals, but none were really pets. I hatched baby snapping turtles from eggs and fed them worms and minnows for several months. I had hand-reared a groundhog, a raccoon, a robin, and a red-headed woodpecker, but all were kept in cages. I wanted a pet; an animal that would accompany me on walks and come when called—an animal that truly enjoyed my companionship.

I wanted a young hawk to raise, but never found a nest located in a tree that could be safely climbed. That never kept me from trying and led to a frightening accident. The spring of 1879, I discovered an active goshawk nest in a massive gray-barked, beech tree growing near the banks of Patterson Creek. After we threw a heavy, fifty-foot hemp rope over the lowest limb I stepped into a loop tied in the end of the rope and Warner and John slowly hoisted me up to the first limb. When assured of my footing, I tossed the rope over the next limb and, with help from Warner and John, eased my way another six feet up.

Suddenly out of the sky rocketed a gray form directly towards my face. I managed to jerk my head sideways and avoid the double set of extended talons, but the parent bird knocked off my hat as it streaked past. Before I had time to recover, I was attacked again. This time I was not so fortunate. The talons raked my left ear and blood spurted onto my neck. I quickly realized goshawks are such ferocious defenders of their young that I was risking my life to continue the pursuit.

I managed to lower myself to the first large limb, slip my right foot in the loop, and signal my brothers to lower me towards safety. However, the goshawk initiated one more dive. This time, sharp talons struck my hand, causing me to release my hold on the rope and plummet to the ground. Warner made an effort to catch me, but only slightly broke my fall. I twisted in mid-air, completing my plunge headfirst. My skull suffered a terrible blow as the back of my head struck a protruding tree root. I was knocked unconscious!

Warner and John carried me home and Dad immediately sent Warner to fetch the doctor from Romney. I regained consciousness on the second day and by the fifth was up and about. My head hurt, but I could move all my fingers and even my toes.

Lizzie told me that she had sat with me day and night, keeping a wet towel on my head and talking to me constantly. She was quite critical of my older brothers, saying they should never encourage me in such dangerous ventures. I was fortunate I had not cracked my skull.

The doctor warned, "Another strong blow to the same spot on your skull could prove fatal."

Knowing my desires, and feeling a little guilty about their role in my fall from the beech, Warner and John searched diligently for a pet. Unable to find an accessible hawk nest, they settled for a crow nest. Warner first spotted the pair of crows carrying sticks into the upper branches of a large hemlock tree at the edge of the pasture. The nest was completed in ten days, and nearly four weeks later the parents began bringing food to their nestlings. Although under strict orders not to climb a tree, I was permitted to observe the crow's feeding visits, which numbered as high as twenty per hour.

Warner learned from a friend at the sawmill that the young crows would leave the nest about forty days after hatching. If I wanted a nestling that would become tame we would need to remove it from the nest when it was no more than three weeks old.

One Saturday morning, we gathered the necessary equipment and the Leatherman family moved en masse to the hemlock tree. Even Lizzie and young Daniel went along. Warner climbed the tree this time, and I observed with the rest of the family from a distance.

Hemlocks growing in an open field typically have branches reaching almost to the ground, thus making them easy to climb. Crow parents do not defend their nests like hawks and owls, making this a much safer climb. Warner reached the nest and lowered a small rope to the ground. John attached a small basket containing a blanket. Warner retrieved the basket and gently lifted the largest nestling from the nest, placed it in the basket, covered it with the blanket, and began lowering it to the ground.

Everyone crowded around as I gingerly lifted the blanket. A set of deep blue eyes peered out curiously, eyes sparkling like the bright sky when a December storm pushes away all the clouds. The nestling showed little fear. Wing and tail feathers were partially developed, and the body was encased in a layer of soft, grayish-black, down feathers.

We had been advised to keep the nestling entrapped in the dark basket for twelve hours before attempting to feed it. Upon removing the blanket the next morning, the nestling immediately began to beg for food. I had been collecting earthworms for a week and when the crow opened its red gape I dropped in a small worm. Five more worms quickly followed. I covered the basket with the blanket and returned it to a high shelf in the barn. Feeding continued at hourly intervals throughout the day, and as darkness fell I was confident the nestling recognized and welcomed me as its sole provider.

On the third day I removed Blackie, as I had named the nestling, from the basket and placed it into a small cage constructed of slender hickory sticks. The bottom was covered with twigs and bark to simulate its former nest and a small side door enabled me to feed worms or small salamanders to it.

Within a week the crow was jumping and flying in place to exercise its wings and emitting begging cries whenever I came into view. When a month old, Blackie hopped onto my hand for the first time. Crows are highly social birds that form strong social bonds and have a deep need for companionship. They live in family groups and will not tolerate living alone. Thus, it was natural for the nestling to bond to me.

At about two months of age, Blackie was following me on walks around the farm and perching on my shoulder. I continued to provide worms, crickets, grasshoppers, and other insects, but Blackie was capable of finding and catching all the food he needed.

We never did know if Blackie was a he or a she, it being impossible to distinguish a male crow from a female. I wanted it to be a male, and referred to it as "he". He would often feed with the free-ranging chickens in the barnyard, competing with them for any small critters they discovered.

By mid-summer the interior of Blackie's mouth had turned a pale gray and he had developed his full adult plumage. Blackie regularly flew around the barn, often landing in trees or on roofs. However, on hearing my distinctive two-note whistle he would swoop down and alight on my shoulder. He tolerated everyone except Zedekiah. Zedekiah frightened Blackie with a large garter snake one day, and the crow never forgot the incident. He would fly up to the barn roof when Zedekiah appeared, and scold raucously until my brother went out of sight.

Blackie enjoyed teasing our barn cats and at times even Ulysses, and would frequently pull their tails when he found them sleeping. He also enjoyed pulling our hair. Unfortunately, one of Blackie's favorite targets was Caroline. The crow would quietly fly down when Caroline was sitting in a chair on the porch or in the yard and grab her long black hair. Caroline would scream, jump from her chair, and fling her arms wildly at the crow. She took to using a broom in her attacks but never managed a solid hit.

One night I overheard Caroline say to my Dad, "That boy causes me so much trouble I want to pull my hair out. But I won't need to because his crow is doing it for me."

I heard Dad laugh lightly, and knew he would not make me get rid of my pet. On numerous occasions Blackie redeemed himself, even in Caroline's eyes. He typically spotted intruders even before Ulyesses did. Soaring chicken hawks were scolded loudly, as were invading skunks, foxes, and opossums.

His greatest contribution was detecting black snakes headed for the chicken house. He would dive at them while emitting his loudest caws. Our family recognized the warning, and hurried to save the eggs. Blackie would fly close overhead, croaking triumphantly as the snake was carried to the barn.

In September, Blackie began making solo flights to the fields and woods, often being absent for days at a time. Reports came to us of a tame crow visiting neighboring farms, and I was certain it was "my" crow. Although Blackie was free to come and go as he pleased, I believed he would never really leave me.

One day in October I watched him join a flock of crows feeding in a picked-over cornfield. When they flew away to roost, he accompanied them. He was gone for almost two months, but on a cold, snowy December day he returned to our farm and landed on the barn roof. Recognizing his repeated caws, I ran outside and was thrilled to have him fly down to my shoulder. He stayed a few hours during which time I fed him some of his favorite treats—dried apple slices, bits of bacon, pumpkin seeds, and shelled pinto beans. However, as darkness approached he flew off to the north, apparently headed for a large crow roost in a white pine grove. He never again paid us a visit and never again sat on my shoulder. I wouldn't have traded him for any other wild animal—not even a goshawk.

One August day, the kind oft referred to as a "dog day of summer," while Lizzie and I were searching for fox grapes, my sister said, "I know something you don't."

"What is it? Tell me what it is! You know we never keep secrets from one another."

Lizzie smugly responded, "It involves Caroline."

I asked, "Is she leaving? Is she sick?"

"No. It's something else. She probably thinks its good news. Dad probably thinks its good news."

I smirked and said, "You know I'm not very good at guessing games. Give me a better hint or just tell me what it is."

Lizzie smiled and stated, "We're going to have another baby in our family."

I immediately asked, "How do you know? Are you sure? Did Caroline tell you?"

Lizzie noted, "I just know! You boys don't notice such things. I saw how our mother changed when she was carrying Daniel and when Caroline was carrying Emma. She now looks and acts exactly the same. I'm positive she'll have another baby in a couple months."

By September, even I could see that Lizzie was right. Dad confirmed this when he announced at supper one night, "Caroline's expecting a child sometime in the next month or two and we're trying to pick a name. If anyone has an idea we want to hear it."

No one said a word. After several awkward moments, Lizzie spoke, "If we knew whether it will be a boy or girl we might be able to make a suggestion."

Nothing more was said about the baby that night. By October Caroline was quite heavy and it seemed to me she would be having her baby any day. On October 12th Dad sent Warner for a doctor from Romney.

We left the house and stayed in the barn while another Leatherman baby was being born. Caroline gave birth to a baby boy on October

13, but it did not live. The boy, named Joseph, was buried near the grave of my Mother.

CHAPTER NINE

The Big Decision

Dad first described to us the place called Canaan the autumn when I was eight. While eating supper, he said, "Remember that land I bought at a sheriff's tax sale a couple year's ago in Tucker County? I saw Solomon Cosner in town today and he heard rumors that in a few years the railroad will be extended up the North Branch from Piedmont to reach the huge coal deposits and stands of timber.

The West Virginia Central and Pittsburg Railroad currently ends near Keyser, about forty miles from the northern end of Canaan Valley. But they've already started expanding the rails toward Tucker County. Once the tracks reach the Canaan area, sawmills, pulp mills, and tanneries will be built, and that area will support the largest logging industry the United States has ever seen. The huge timber will make someone very rich, and there'll be thousands of new jobs. "

Dad continued, "It's an amazing place. The trees are huge, so gigantic it took five days for two men with a cross-cut saw to topple one to the ground."

Warner, always the clever one, piped up, "Those men are so lazy they should be fired, or someone should show them how to sharpen their saw."

Zedekiah and I chuckled, while a slight grin appeared on Dad's face. He continued, "Solomon said there's more timber growing in the Canaan area than any place he has ever seen in his life. There are no sawmills, and the only trees cut so far were used to build a few log cabins and barns. The forest stretches at least one hundred square miles. The black cherry trees are so massive the first limbs are at least 100 feet above the ground."

As long as I could remember, my father had been a land speculator. He bought and sold several large tracts in Mineral County, and purchased the timber rights on others. He was familiar with the Canaan Valley area and outlined the financial rewards our family could gain if we were to own timber in the Canaan area.

Later that winter, Dad again brought up the subject of Canaan. As we ate supper he revealed some of his thoughts, "The Baltimore and Ohio will finish rebuilding the bridges along their railroad lines this winter. Most of the big timber around Hampshire and Mineral counties has been cut, and once it's gone we'll most likely lose our jobs. I've been thinking seriously about Canaan, and decided we should move there before the railroad arrives."

With obvious enthusiasm, Dad added, "Solomon Cosner sent word that there's a nice spot for a cabin along a small stream he named Sand Run, on one of the tracts I bought at the tax sale. Although much of the surrounding lowland is boggy, that along the elevated middle ridge is gently rolling and more inviting than the surrounding rocky mountainsides.

"There's no lack of trees for building cabins and barns, and the sandy, well-drained soils will grow crops. There's a large natural glade that grows grass as high as a man's head every summer. Also, there are herds of wild horses and cattle that have survived in the valley since the Civil War."

Dad continued, "Four families live in Canaan: Solomon Cosner, who owns 850 acres, John Nine, with 500 acres, James Freeland, with about 300 acres, and Robert Eastham, with 500 acres. We can't depart until the snow is gone from the mountains, but, if we're going, we should leave by May. We'll thus have time to plant a garden, build a cabin and a barn, and cut enough hay to supply our livestock, plus shoot and dry our winter-supply of meat. We can take a wagon, although Cosner reported there is only one road leading over the mountain."

I overheard Dad tell Warner and John, while they were milking, that Canaan was a real wilderness. You could walk for miles and never see evidence that man had been there. Wild animals roamed freely, with timber wolves, mountain lions, and black bears seen regularly.

Dad said, "You boys better get a couple more hunting dogs before we leave. Old Ulysses won't be able to handle all those ferocious critters by himself. Also, you better try to buy another good hunting rifle to take with us.

"You should be able to collect enough hides and furs from the Canaan wilderness to buy the things we can't grow or harvest. We'll need to tan several bearskins to keep us warm during winter. Solomon said the winters can be something fierce, with a whole lot more snow, ice, and cold temperatures than we have ever seen in the South Branch Valley."

I listened wide-eyed in silent awe, realizing I would be seeing animals I had never before encountered and would certainly need my own gun. If I got a job at the sawmill where Dad and the boys worked I could earn enough money to buy an old used rifle and some shells. Although I was fascinated by wild animals and looked forward to raising many more as pets, my goal was to be a famous hunter. I was so excited I couldn't wait to tell Lizzie.

Then Dad told my brothers, "Maybe we better not tell Caroline about the wild animals and the wilderness and the bad winters. She doesn't seem all that excited about leaving her family and taking baby Emma across the mountains."

I changed my mind about telling Lizzie, figuring she wouldn't be nearly as excited as I was. However, I planned to ask Dad about getting me a job at the sawmill. Zedekiah had started working there when he was nine years old, carrying water, moving sawn boards, and feeding horses. I was confident I could do that and more.

When the snow melted from the South Branch Valley we began making plans in earnest for moving to Canaan. I had been working at the sawmill for nearly two months and had earned enough money to buy a rifle.

After much searching and spreading the word that I was in the market for a boy-sized rifle, we located an old single-shot Sharps cavalry carbine with shortened stock. The owner, Nicholas Arnold, said that particular breech-loading Sharps rifle had been used at the battle of Bull Run during the Civil War, and it had killed several hundred bluecoats. He had nearly three-dozen cartridges that he would throw in with the sale. I was convinced it was just the right rifle for me, capable of dropping a deer or bear or charging mountain lion.

However, Warner offered some valuable advice, "You won't be able to buy cartridges for the Sharps in the Canaan wilderness, and without cartridges the rifle will be worthless. Why don't we try to find an old muzzleloader that the owner abandoned for a more modern, cartridge-shooting rifle? There must be hundreds leaning in the corners of barns or hanging from rafters in the houses around the South Branch Valley.

"Cartridge rifles would certainly be preferred if you were fighting in a war, because of the ease of loading and reloading. However, if you're hunting wild game, your rifle will be loaded before you begin your stalk. Most importantly, it will be a whole lot easier to buy lead and black powder than to buy manufactured cartridges. By melting the lead over a fire, you can form bullets of the right caliber in the bullet mold that comes with the muzzleloader."

In late February Warner came home with a medium-sized 35-caliber muzzleloader, which he bought for only two dollars. Owned by one of the Kercheval boys in Romney, it was in excellent condition. Included in the deal were a powder horn, a bullet mold, a leather bag of black powder, and another of lead bullets. The rifle had originally been a flintlock, but had been modified to use caps to ignite the powder in the barrel. Fortunately for us, Kercheval still had the flintlock mechanism and gave it to Warner.

The barrel was nearly four feet long, and I had to prop it in a tree crotch or across a fallen log to hold it steady. At first I practiced holding it steady without actually firing, imagining that I was sighting a bear or huge buck. I began to carry it with me when hiking or looking for bird nests, and slowly became comfortable with it in my hands, although I could not carry it for any length of time without stopping to rest. Both Warner and John fired it several times and proclaimed, mainly for my benefit, that it was the most accurate gun they had ever shot.

Finally, one spring-like day in March, I fired it for the first time. The stock slammed into my shoulder so hard I thought it must be broken.

Tears came to my eyes. I was a skinny boy, with no extra muscle on my bones. After that initial firing, I wore a jacket with hay packed into the shoulder for padding and learned that if I held the stock tight against my shoulder the kick would be tolerable.

With guidance from Warner, I was soon able to hit a tree trunk at fifty yards; of course, the tree had to have a four-foot diameter. In my mind, I was a real sharpshooter. The muzzleloader was usually reliable, although on a few occasions the bullet stuck in the barrel and we had to ream it out.

Another problem occurred when I poured too much black powder down the gun barrel. I was usually careful and added no more than would cover the lead bullet in the palm of my hand. However, one day when distracted while loading the rifle I put a second load of powder down the barrel. Fortunately for me the rifle was well constructed and no damage resulted. Caroline listened while Zedekiah described the incident at the supper table and harshly warned, "That ole gun will blow your head off someday."

Dad had decided we would depart for Canaan in April, allowing two weeks to make the trip. Lizzie, with Zedekiah's assistance, prepared a list of everything we would take, and estimated how much space each item would require. Clothing, cooking/eating utensils, kettles, crocks, buckets, and butter churns were first on the list. Axes, saws, augers, shovels, scythes, and ropes were equally essential. Many of the smaller items could be packed in wooden barrels.

Tables, benches, and beds would be dismantled and piled neatly in the bottom of the wagon. Oaken baskets would be packed tightly with dried roots of medicinal plants—sassafras, echinacea, goldenseal, black cohosh, May apple, and many others. A barrel of flour and one of cornmeal were essential if we were to have pies, cakes, and cornbread. Even more important than flour and cornmeal, was salt. We would need at least two barrels. Everything we ate needed salt, and without salt much of our meat would spoil. Salt would also be essential in drying the furs and hides we accumulated.

Lizzie calculated that everything we needed would fit in our wagon—until Caroline insisted we take the big wood-fired cook stove. Dad said there was no way we could take that monstrosity, but Caroline didn't give in. She firmly stated, "I'll not cook over the open flames in a hot, smoky fireplace. And, without the cook stove there'll be no biscuits, or bread, or pies."

The thought of life without hot biscuits shocked all of us, including Dad. We could give up a lot of luxuries, but none of us wanted to imagine such a major sacrifice. We all looked appealingly at Dad, and he proposed, "There's no way we can take the big cook stove, but possibly we can find a small one that will fit in the wagon."

Warren said, "Don't forget, we need to buy a couple new rifles, several boxes of ammunition, and a dozen steel traps."

Lizzie shocked everyone when she interjected, "But first you must get a stone marker for Mom's grave. If you don't get a carved stone, I'll have to stay here and take care of her wooden marker. You can go without me."

It was evident that Dad was a little dismayed and much perturbed. He didn't like people telling him what to do, but it was evident some hard decisions had to be made.

Caroline didn't help matters when she pronounced, "Everyone agrees we must have a cook stove. Besides, you already have three rifles, and certainly can do without another for a few months. And, you could place a new carved oak board at the grave, and come back later and put up a nice permanent stone monument. Memories of her life won't depend on a sculpted stone, but on her children who recite tales of her life to their own children."

Lizzie frowned deeply and Dad's face revealed frustration. It was obvious Caroline did not realize how far from civilization we would be living and how essential the new rifles and traps were. Lizzie, quietly but firmly reminded Dad, "You made a deathbed promise, sealed with a kiss, to get a stone marker!"

Suddenly the cabin became still, and for nearly ten minutes no one spoke. Gradually, it was silently agreed that a permanent stone marker must be erected before we left. A crude wooden slab was not adequate for the brave women who had been such an important part of our lives.

Another concern of moving to Canaan was the lack of a school. My older brothers had attended public school for several years and could read and write. But Lizzie and I had one year of school so far.

The one-room, log schoolhouse was a little over two miles from our cabin and Zedekiah, Lizzie, and I walked there every morning and returned every evening. School was held during October and November, when there was not much work for us to do around the farm and when the weather was not too severe. Free public education was available to persons six to twenty-one years old, and Mom had insisted that all of her children attend.

The teacher, a Mr. Staggs, taught all eighteen students, ranging in age from six to nineteen. The rough floor of our school was constructed of slabs cut from massive tulip popular logs. Seats and log benches were of split poplar logs. The building was heated with a huge pot-bellied stove. Mr. Staggs used the New Testament for reading lessons, and small hand-held chalkboards for number's lessons. We had turkey quill pens, but usually no writing paper to practice making our letters.

Mr. Staggs would often read a verse from the New Testament, and then have a student read it again after he was finished. Zedekiah helped Lizzie and me at home after school and by the end of the school term we were able to read many words and a few verses in the Bible.

Although Lizzie was a slow reader, she was one of the brightest students in class when it came to doing her numbers. I thought Lizzie would make a great teacher and often wondered, after my untimely death, whether she ended up as the primary teacher in a one-room schoolhouse.

One dreary, overcast Saturday in early April, Dad returned from a trip to Romney with a gravestone for Mom. It was about one foot wide and two feet high. When placed in the ground, the visible portion was one foot square. The carved inscription read, "Mary Leatherman, wife of George. Born 1835, died 1875."

After church the next day, the entire family, including Caroline and baby Emma, slowly trudged to Mom's grave. Dad silently replaced the wooden marker with the stone one. He then set the wooden marker at the foot of the grave, so that each end was prominently marked. Mom's spirit surely rejoiced to see that finely sculpted stone set upon her grave.

Each member of the family, other than Caroline and Emma, in turn said a few words, expressing their gratitude for everything she had done to establish the solid foundation for our family. We all realized that we would likely never revisit her gravesite once we left for the Canaan wilderness.

I wish I had known that in ten months my body would be resting in a similar grave. I would have told her how much I missed her, and that I was sorry for all the troubles I had caused. I would have planted trilliums, Jack-in-the-pulpits, pink lady slippers, and bleeding hearts on her grave. She always enjoyed flowers and her spirit would have been greatly pleased to view the showy blooms each summer.

Chapter Ten

Over The Allegheny

As the sun rose over Mill Point Mountain the second week of April 1880, our caravan departed our Mineral County homestead. We each had personal regrets, but other than Caroline we eagerly anticipated this grand adventure. Undoubtedly, I was the most excited of all. I had my own rifle and would be hunting and trapping animals, confident of shooting a wolf, a mountain lion, and probably even a bear or two.

I could anticipate being the designated hunter for the Leatherman clan. Dad and my older brothers would be too busy cutting trees, building a cabin and barn, and harvesting hay to have time to hunt. Although the largest animal I had killed with my muzzleloader was a groundhog, I had no doubt I could easily kill a deer if we needed the meat.

Spring had arrived in the Potomac Valley, and we were fortunate to begin our trip in near-perfect weather. Cardinals, robins, red-winged blackbirds, and a multitude of other birds filled the crisp air with their joyful singing. Trilliums were blooming on rich, damp hillsides and May apples were pushing their bright green leaves towards the treetops. Maples, tulip poplars, and sassafras were also unfurling their leaves.

With the sun to our backs, we followed a small road west to Patterson Creek where we picked up the well-traveled road that headed southwest between Mill Creek Mountain and Knobly Mountain towards Petersburg. The valley was about five miles wide and travel was easy, with no steep grades to climb. Caroline, Daniel, and little Emma rode in the overloaded, high-wheeled wagon.

Our three unhappy milk cows were tied to the back of the wagon, and forced to plod along at a speed matching that of the horses. The two-dozen chickens were crammed in four small cages tied to the sides of the wagon. Dad, Warner, and John walked in front of the horses, watching for rattlesnakes and copperheads, while Zedekiah, Lizzie, and I brought up the rear. Our three dogs, Ulysses, Fury, and Ranger wandered as they pleased, frequently running out of sight in search of some critter they had sighted or scented.

The cacophony created by our caravan was so loud we could hardly hear each other talking. Leather harnesses squeaked, kettles banged, barrels rattled, tools thudded, chickens squawked, and dogs barked, while Daniel and Emma laughed and squealed when the wagon clattered over a bump.

We passed seven farmhouses that first day, and at each one the inhabitants heard us long before they saw us. Two or three children would typically run to the road and ask where we were headed. Not far behind them would be an adult, also curious. Eager to hear news, we usually stopped and tried to answer their questions.

We covered the thirty miles from our farm to Petersburg in three days, spending the first night in a large hay barn at the invite of a family named Kerns and the second in a barn owned by the Crites family. The road was in decent condition and the four-foot high wheels of our wagon rolled smoothly over bumps and through mud holes. Although Patterson Creek diminished in size as we neared its headwaters, we had no trouble catching enough fish for everyone to eat their fill each evening. The fishing poles were strapped to the side of the wagon, as were the rifles, easily accessible if needed in a hurry.

The second day of our journey our hounds treed an opossum, which was brought tumbling to the ground by a shot from Warner. The hounds also treed two plump gray squirrels, which Zedekiah dropped. Fried fish accompanied roasted possum and squirrel that evening.

A couple miles north of Petersburg the road crossed over a small divide and we picked up the North Fork of the South Branch of the Potomac. The valley narrowed noticeably at this point, but the wagon road was straight and smooth enough that we still made good time. By the fourth day, the mountains were pinching in on us. North Fork

Mountain on the east rose to 3,500 feet, while the Allegheny Front on the west reached nearly 4,500 feet.

Although spring had arrived in the Potomac Valley, the gray, leafless trees covering the mountaintops indicated that winter still maintained its grip on the higher elevations. Snowdrifts were visible on the shady, north-facing peaks, ominous signs that our journey over the Allegheny Front would not be so gentle and enjoyable as that along the South Branch.

On the morning of the fifth day we spotted numerous, near-vertical cliffs and huge rock slides accentuating the rugged mountain ridges. Although Canaan Valley lay nearly due west of our current location, Dad explained we must move a few miles farther south before we could turn west and successfully cross the Allegheny Front.

Towards evening a huge towering mass of rock, situated east of the river came into view. The cliffs and rockslides extended from the eastern bank of the South Branch River to a height exceeding that of all adjoining ridges. It was the most spectacular rock formation we had ever seen. We camped in the bottomland across the river from the rocks, known locally as Seneca Rocks, aware that the easy part of our journey had ended.

Warner and John wanted to try to climb Seneca Rocks, but the South Branch River was running high due to snowmelt in the mountains, and they could not safely cross. With rays of the setting sun illuminating the tips of the enormous sandstone formation, we stared in awe at the wondrous sights. Lizzie reverently stated, "That is the most amazing thing I have ever seen. I wish I were a painter so that I could show other people the golden peaks that miraculously appear at sundown."

The scene was not so spectacular the next morning, because the sun rose almost directly behind the formation. Although still impressive, it now appeared sinister and almost threatening as the west face was in dark shadow.

Dad explained that for the next couple days we would follow a small side valley that climbed up into the foothills bordering the Allegheny Front. The trail was prominent, but had felt the wheels of very few wagons. We followed Seneca Creek for the remainder of that day, climbing gradually towards the only gap that offered access across the Allegheny Front.

After covering only four miles we established camp near a farmstead situated in the bottomland where Roaring Creek merged with Seneca Creek. The site would later be known as Onego. On several occasions that day, fallen trees across the trail brought our travel to a temporary halt. Each time, Dad, Warner, and John cleared the path for the wagon. It was apparent that the primary travelers on this trail had been men on horseback, because the detours wove among trees growing too close to one another for a wagon to maneuver.

While Warner, John, and Dad wielded axe and crosscut saw to clear the road, Zedekiah and I fished every deep pool we could find. Other than small creek chubs, the only fish we caught were brook trout. Although most were less than twelve inches in length, they were fun to catch and a sight to behold. Red spots, with blue circles, were liberally scattered over their sides, and the reddish lower fins were strikingly bordered with white along their leading edge.

Because brook trout had such small scales it was not necessary to scale and filet them as we did the suckers and fallfish. After gutting, the entire fish was dropped into a skillet of hot grease and left to sizzle for two to three minutes before being turned. In another two minutes it was ready for a pre-warmed tin plate.

When cooked, the pink brook trout flesh could be readily separated from each side of the skeleton, and the filets were eaten with no concern for bones. Even Daniel and little Emma were given large chunks of fish with no worry about choking. Brook trout and stick bread comprised our evening meal many evenings of our journey, and all agreed they were one of the highlights of our journey.

The next day's travel was even more difficult. Although the grade was not steep, the number of trees obstructing the path created constant delays. Dad, Warner, and John wielded the cross-cut saw for hours at a time, one resting while the other two attempted to move the saw back and forth through the targeted tree. Covering only a few hundred feet at a time, we followed Seneca Creek until it forked, at which juncture we set up camp for the night. Dad estimated that we had covered only three miles that day.

During one delay that afternoon, Zedekiah and I had gone hunting. It was evident that several hours would be required to clear the wagon road, so we went out trying to supplement the menu for the evening meal. The forest was dominated by huge chestnuts and even larger oaks, providing nearly perfect habitat for gray squirrel.

My brother and I moved as a team around the mountainside, usually separated by ten to thirty yards. A squirrel that spotted one of us would typically skirt around the tree trunk to avoid detection, giving the other one of us a clear shot. Our strategy worked, and Zedekiah was able to shoot three squirrels.

I had one good opportunity. Unfortunately, I didn't have a convenient spot to rest my rifle and the wobbling barrel assured the squirrel would live to see another day.

About one hour after our hunt began, Zedekiah spooked a gray squirrel and it ran around the tree, skirted up the trunk, and stretched out on one of the tree's lower limbs. I was beside a fallen tree when I spotted the squirrel and thus had an ideal resting pad for my rifle. Carefully taking aim, I slowly squeezed the trigger. Gunpowder exploded and a small cloud of smoke screened my view. However, no sound of a dead squirrel striking the ground was heard.

I was so disgusted that I almost threw my gun down. Disappointment turned to joy when the smoke finally cleared and I spotted the squirrel lying awkwardly across the limb. Apparently my shot had not struck it solid enough to propel it from the limb.

The tree was a mid-sized white oak, only fifteen inches in diameter. I didn't want to abandon my first squirrel, but knew a second shot would probably make it unfit to eat. I convinced Zedekiah that, with his assistance, I could shinny up the tree. I climbed onto his shoulders and then wrapped my arms and legs around the tree trunk.

Slowly but surely I inched up the tree. A small limb growing opposite the one supporting the squirrel provided a firm handhold for my left hand and I reached up to grasp my very first gray squirrel. But triumph quickly changed to shock—and major pain. The squirrel had been grazed by my bullet, not killed. At my touch, it sank its teeth deeply into my thumb. I screamed wildly, while grasping the tree tightly with my legs and one free hand. The more I shook my hand, the deeper the squirrel bit. I could feel its long, sharp teeth hit the bone.

Zedekiah, remembering my previous fall and the doctor's warning about another head injury, yelled at me to hold on. I wasn't certain what suggestions he was making because of his near-hysterical laughter. I heard Zedekiah yell, between laughs, "Bite it! Bite it! Bite the squirrel!"

Slowly it registered in my frightened brain that the squirrel had no intentions of releasing its grip on my thumb. Pulling it close to my face, I clamped my teeth solidly onto its tail. When nothing happened I began grinding my teeth back and forth across the tailbone. I nearly choked from the mouthful of hair but resolved not to stop. Seconds later the squirrel released its hold and fell to the ground. Zedekiah was able to clamp his boot onto the squirrel's head and my first squirrel was finally bagged.

We headed back towards the wagon, and Zedekiah killed two more squirrels. Six squirrels would provide enough meat for our family and we proudly rejoined the family. While Zedekiah and I had been hunting, Lizzie had been digging ramps. These aromatic wild onions send up their elongated green leaves each spring, often while late snows blanket the forest floor. Their strategy is to send forth leaves before the tree canopy closes, at which time there is typically not enough sunlight to survive.

After washing the loose soil from the bulbous roots, the entire plants, six to ten inches long, were gently dropped into a skillet of hot grease over our evening cooking fire. When the green leaves had darkened, ramps joined grilled squirrel on each tin plate and the feast began.

After eating, Zedekiah described my encounter with the wounded gray squirrel. He declared it to be, absolutely, the funniest thing he had ever seen in his life. My thumb hurt like the devil, and I didn't think it was the least bit funny! I announced proudly, "I killed my very first squirrel, and nothing else matters."

The right fork of Seneca Creek tended northwest, our desired direction of travel. Unfortunately, that more direct route would have forced us to climb one of the highest ridges along the Alleghenies. Instead, we followed the more prominent, southward leading fork. A light rain began falling around mid-day, and travel slowed even more. Everyone pulled on a rain slicker and an oiled canvas was secured over the wagon. We covered only two miles before darkness forced us to stop for the night. Instead of tasty brook trout or grilled gray squirrel we had dried beef, a little warm milk, and nothing else. Although enough, we all longed for hot biscuits or skillet fried corn bread.

Caroline, Emma, Daniel, Lizzie, Zedekiah, and I slept under the wagon, which was six feet wide and nearly twenty feet long. Dad, Warner, and John built a lean-to of spruce limbs against one side of the wagon and covered it with an oiled canvas. That provided adequate shelter for them, and prevented the rain from blowing in under the wagon.

We complained about being cramped, although I enjoyed the cozy arrangement. Dad repeated tales of free-ranging cattle and horses that roamed throughout Canaan Valley, and assured us we would have no trouble obtaining adequate beef to feed the entire family. I would have liked a campfire, but the steady light rain on the canvas created a setting almost as enjoyable as a fire.

The rain continued throughout the night and by mid-morning had turned to a wet, slushy snow. We couldn't believe it. The grade steepened noticeably, and it became necessary to assist the horses. Dad walked slightly behind the team, urging them with loud commands and a hickory switch. Warner and John pushed against the spokes of the two front wheels, while Zedekiah and I were assigned the rear wheels. Caroline carried Emma, and Lizzie led Daniel.

Trees became noticeably smaller as we pushed ever higher, and by mid-afternoon stunted spruce, beech, and deciduous holly became prevalent. With the ominous dark clouds pressing upon us, and heavy wet snow falling steadily, we lost the trail. Dad announced that we would stop for the night. Once again we ate dried beef with warm milk under the shelter of the wagon.

Whereas the previous night had been somewhat enjoyable this one was barely tolerable. Even with wool blankets, it was necessary for us to snuggle together to keep warm. We had already celebrated the arrival of spring in the South Branch Valley, and summer couldn't be too far behind. We shouldn't be having snow this late in the year. For the first time, we expressed doubts about our journey. If we had not been so exhausted from pushing the wagon we probably would not have slept. But, tired bodies ignore the cold when in need of restoration.

Daylight brought one of those scenes almost too spectacular to describe. The storm had passed and the sun was glaring off a blanket of brilliant snow. Every twig, limb, and tree trunk bore a white coating, and the air was filled with twisting, twirling ice crystals. The cold Canadian air had swept out the snow clouds and dropped the temperature into the teens.

We fed the chickens, cows, and horses double rations of grain and fed ourselves more dried beef. Although milk production had dropped drastically, Warner and John were able to coax enough from our cows to provide a warm cup for everyone in the family. The combination of cold weather and being cramped in the small cage brought a near halt to egg production by our chickens. We found only two eggs in the cages that morning.

The biggest surprise was not the snow, which we had expected, but the discovery that we had gained the summit the previous afternoon. Before us stretched a broad open plain, dotted with shrubs, stunted trees, and numerous wagon-sized boulders. Winds had swept the snow from large patches of grasses that dominated this high mountain bald. Although it was cold and snow-covered, the grass was eagerly consumed by our hungry livestock.

With animals and people fed, we were ready to begin our descent. However, we faced one serious problem. The snow had obliterated any trace of the trail. We could stay put until the snow melted. We could head west; reasoning that as we dropped off the summit the snow cover would lighten and eventually disappear. Or, Dad and the older boys could go in search of the trail while the rest of us gathered enough firewood to build a fire.

Cosner had informed Dad that upon crossing the summit, a distinct, forested, narrow-sided drainage would lead us off the mountain. White's Run, a small mountain brook, tumbled down the drainage, eventually reaching the Dry Fork River. Once we found the drainage and the associated White's Run, it would be a simple matter of following it until we reached the Dry Fork River, less than three miles away. Dad decided to begin the gradual descent, so we might escape the blowing snow and chilling north wind.

Although we had to skirt snowdrifts reaching nearly six feet tall, we moved steadily. Where possible, Dad guided the horses onto stretches void of snow, and the wagon moved easily across the frozen sod. In less than one hour we were in the shelter of full-size trees and a short time later we located a westward trickling stream. Dad brought the wagon to a halt near a small stand of spruce and ordered the older boys to gather tree limbs while we youngsters gathered enough small twigs and spruce knots to start a fire. Unlike most trees, spruce keep their lower dead branches, and that dry, dead wood provided excellent fuel for our fire. With our bodies warmed externally by the flames and internally by the cups of sassafras tea our spirits soared.

Dad said we had conquered the worst. We all knew it would not be easy, but desperately wanted to believe there would be no more snowstorms.

With bodies and minds refreshed, Dad, Warner, and John went in search of the trail. Zedekiah, Lizzie, and I used a small axe to cut more dead spruce limbs, while Caroline prepared stick bread. After mixing flour, baking powder, and two eggs she kneaded the dough into a ball and rolled it into long slender strips. These we wrapped around slender, four-foot long maple limbs stripped of twigs and then held them over the small cooking fire. They were delicious!

Less than one hour after they departed, Dad and my brothers returned. They were surprised to be handed cups of hot sassafras tea and swirls of stick bread. Warner announced they had found a distinct trail and were positive it would lead us gently down to the Dry Fork.

Unfortunately, winter storms had dropped many trees across the trail, and the sound of axes and crosscut saws filled the air for most of that afternoon. After we had covered less than one mile we entered dense mature hardwood timber where the snow was only a couple inches deep. We again slept under the wagon, with a lean-to sheltering the windward side. By snuggling together we remained comfortable if not cozy.

Late the next morning, while our two new hounds, Fury and Ranger, were off hunting, Ulysses was sniffing around the top of a large tulip poplar that had toppled. His deep, exaggerated howls made us suspect he had located a large animal. John quickly retrieved his Sharp's rifle, and Dad, Warner, Zedekiah, and I joined him in a rapid race to the downed tree.

Warner found a large rock, nearly as big as a loaf of bread, and threw it into the branches. Suddenly, a big black animal came running out the other side and started up the hill. Ulysses immediately started in pursuit and in less than fifty yards had caught up with the animal, a yearling black bear. Ulysses caught the bear by one of its hind legs, the bear squealed in fright, and dog and bear rolled down the hill.

I was certain the bear would cause serious injury to Ulysses. While they were rolling downhill, John was running as fast as he could to catch up with them. The bear broke loose from Ulysses and started running away, but the hound quickly caught up and once again grabbed it by the leg. Eventually the bear escaped and clawed its way up a tree.

The bear had climbed to a limb about sixty feet off the ground when we reached the trunk. With no hesitation, John carefully rested the barrel of his Sharps rifle against a nearby tree trunk and slowly squeezed the trigger. The gunpowder exploded, the lead bullet spiraled out of the barrel, and the bear released its grip on the tree. It tumbled to the ground and Ulysses immediately inflicted two sharp bites. It was dead before hitting the ground.

We crowded around the bear, which Dad estimated to weigh ninety pounds. Warner returned to the wagon to retrieve a rope. Dad and John had just finished gutting the bear when Warner and the rest of the family returned. With the rope tied around one of the bear's hind legs we all shared the task of dragging it back to the wagon. I was disappointed that I had not been given the opportunity to shoot the bear, but figured I would shoot an even bigger one in Canaan Valley.

Everyone was talking anxiously about the bear steaks we would soon be enjoying. But the excitement was not yet over. Ulysses had returned to the downed treetop and started his wild barking again. John reloaded the rifle and we returned to the tree. Warner threw another rock into the mass of limbs but nothing came out. We were skirting around the perimeter of the thick branches when I spotted a large black shape with two small beady eyes.

I proudly announced my find and upon closer inspection we concluded it was the mother bear, possibly with another yearling. These bears had only recently come out of hibernation. Why she didn't run we couldn't imagine. I wanted to shoot it, but Dad said we did not have space to haul the carcass of a full-grown bear.

Warner gripped Ulysses by the collar and dragged him back to the camp where he was secured. By that time our other two hounds had returned, and they likewise were tied to a tree.

After bringing the bear carcass to the back of the wagon, out of reach of the hounds, we built a small cooking fire and all joined in to grill small pieces of bear heart and liver. The few small pieces that each of us consumed only barely whetted our appetite and increased our expectations of the juicy steaks we would enjoy that night.

We made steady progress, in spite of having to lead the cows, which refused to get close to the bear. By evening we had reached relatively flat bottomland. The Dry Fork River was not visible but we knew it could not be far away.

Dad, Warner, and John skinned the bear, careful not to make cuts in the hide, and hung the carcass off the ground beneath a large hemlock tree. In this position, it was easy to slice off steaks and backstrap, which we grilled in skillets and on sharpened sticks over the fire. For the first time on our journey, everyone had more than enough to eat.

CHAPTER ELEVEN

Dry Fork And Red Creek

We ate grilled bear steaks again the next morning. The bear hide, which we would later tan to make a bed for Emma, was tied to the top of the wagon, the bear carcass was tied to the rear, and again we led the cows a short distance behind the wagon.

Around mid-morning we heard the gurgling of the Dry Fork and shortly thereafter, the small settlement of Job came into view. The waters glided smoothly around and over large rocks, before slamming into protruding boulders. Rapids were prevalent and a little daunting. Fortunately, we did not have to cross at that point.

At the invitation of a farmer named Cross, we joined his family for supper in their two-room cabin and talked until long after midnight. They were eager to hear about changes in the South Branch Valley, and we were desirous of anything we could learn about Canaan Valley.

Cross explained how several settlers had moved their horses and cattle into the valley during the Civil War to prevent troops of both sides from claiming them. The valley was so remote that soldiers rarely visited, and no major roads passed nearby. Cross and his neighbors along the Dry Fork had moved twelve horses and over thirty head of cattle into the valley. Hundreds more were driven there from Red Creek, Parsons, and even a few South Branch settlements, but few had remained after the war. Wolves and cougars killed many and those that survived had become wild.

Cross felt that any animals we captured were our property, because more than a decade had passed since their release and most attempts by settlers to retrieve them had failed.

He also suggested that, come autumn, we should plan to shoot a couple of the beef cattle to provide meat for that winter. I didn't say anything, but I secretly anticipated eating meat of bear and deer, not cattle. I wasn't going to Canaan to shoot a cow.

The next morning we departed and the Dry Fork River, which flowed north, guided us ever closer to Canaan Valley. Two days later, we reached the junction of Dry Fork and Red Creek. Dad decided we would camp that night on the south side of Red Creek, and cross the next morning.

Late the next morning we found the rocky ford that Cross had described and judged the water would reach the horse's bellies. With Warner tugging on one horse's bridle and John tugging on the other, Dad loudly urged the horses into Red Creek. The rest of us stood on the creek bank, calling out encouragement. Mac stumbled over a submerged boulder, but regained his footing and continued across the stream. Warner, John, and the horses eased up the opposite bank, followed by Dad and the wagon. We all cheered loudly at the successful crossing.

After unhitching the horses, Warner and John rode them back across Red Creek. With Zedekiah and me as passengers, we crossed over to the wagon. Warner and John made three more trips, during which Caroline, Daniel, Lizzie, Emma, and the cows were safely transported. With no one to hold them back, the three dogs leaped into the water, and dog paddled to the wagon.

Because Dad, Warner, and John had gotten wet, we built a fire to dry their clothes. We once again enjoyed a meal of grilled bear steaks while sitting around a comforting blaze.

Dad's, Warner's, and John's clothes had dried by the time we finished eating, although their boots were still wet. When warmth had returned to their legs we eagerly resumed our northward trek. As we left, Dad was alarmed to notice that Mac was limping. Fortunately the trail at this point was smooth, and the grade was slight. Mac was able to continue, although it appeared that Abe was pulling more than his share.

In late afternoon we reached the Stringtown settlement, and accepted an invite to eat with the John Wolford family. After supper we were joined by the Ebenezer Flanagan family, and with a crowd so large that many had to stand, we garnered more details about the remainder of our journey to Canaan.

In less than two miles the road would exit the Dry Fork drainage and we would encounter the headwaters of the Blackwater River. At that point the terrain would become relatively level and we should easily reach the Freeland farm, and a little farther on the Cosner farm. However, they cautioned, we had one last steep grade to negotiate before reaching the valley. It was only a few hundred yards in length, but was steeper than the grade where we crossed the Allegheny Front.

The Stringtown settlement would be about a day's travel from our farm along Sand Run, and we asked the Wolfords and Flanagans to come visit us later that spring. Dad said, "I'm sure we can use a little help raising logs for the cabin and barn, and company is always welcome."

After a short night in the Wolford's barn we joined their family for a hearty breakfast, after which we continued toward the summit overlooking Canaan Valley. We were happy to note that Mac was not favoring his right foot when we departed. However, in less than an hour his limp returned. With the steep grade facing us, Dad expressed doubt that Mac and Abe could pull the wagon to the top.

Once again, Dad loudly urged the horses to lean into their traces, while Warner and John applied force to the front wheels and the rest of the family pushed against the rear of the wagon. We had covered less than twenty yards when Dad brought the team to a halt. He explained that we could not risk injuring Mac. Without two healthy horses we could never skid enough logs to construct our cabin and barn.

It now became apparent that both horses were exhausted. Although they had been given frequent rests during our travel from the South Branch, the over-loaded wagon had worn them out. Several days might be required for them to recover, if given rest and unlimited amounts of forage to eat.

Dad proposed that we unload at least half our belongings from the wagon. With that done he felt the two horses could haul the lighter wagon to the ridge overlooking Canaan. He explained, "We'll then completely unload the wagon and return for the items we unloaded here. After a second trip up over the steep grade we'll once again pile all our goods onto the wagon and resume our journey."

Warner suggested, "Why don't we go back to Stringtown and see if they'll loan us a horse?"

Dad answered, "You know how contrary Abe is. We've never been able to pair him with a horse other than Mac, and I don't think we'll be successful in finding one anyhow. Every farmer is busy trying to get ground plowed in preparation for spring planting."

We all knew that Dad was too proud to ask for help if there was even the slightest chance we could accomplish the task ourselves.

John then proposed, "If Abe and Mac can haul a few of our belongings to the top we can build a transport sled and move the rest of the goods. Remember that handy sled we built of slender poplar logs? It would be easy to pile the iron kettles, barrels, crocks, and boxes on top, and Abe could pull the sled by himself. We'll need to make three or four trips, but Abe would have no trouble with such light loads."

Caroline had lost any enthusiasm she might have had for the trip, and urged, "Why don't we leave the wagon here, return to the Stringtown settlement, and camp there for a few days in one of their barns. Mac's injured foot can recover and both horses will regain some of their lost strength."

It was obvious that everyone—other than Caroline—was eager to reach Canaan Valley. I was eager to launch my career as a big-game hunter, and did not want to waste several days sitting around an old barn. My older brothers were equally eager to put their hunting skills to a test and begin exploring the mysterious land awaiting us. Dad wanted to get started on construction of our cabin and barn.

Warner argued, "We mustn't do anything that threatens the health of the horses. I've been responsible for the horses the past two years and feel strongly that we must give them several days rest."

After several minutes of silence, Dad announced, "Warner's right. We'll hobble the horses and cows and let them graze here for a couple days. There's enough new grass growing in this little cove to provide their fill, and several small spring-fed streams to supply drinking water. Warner, John, and I will work on clearing the road up to the summit in the meantime."

Caroline firmly said, "Dark clouds are rolling in from the south. We're less than one hour from the Wolford's and I'm sure they won't mind if a few of us spend a couple more nights in their barn. I'll take Lizzie, Daniel, and Emma. You can send one of the boys to get us when you feel the horses have recovered."

Dad ordered Zedekiah and me to accompany them and carry enough food to last three days. We were to return and watch after the animals while he and my two older brothers were clearing the wagon road. I beamed with pride when he stated, "You two boys are good rifle shots and I know you can protect the animals from bears or mountain lions."

We returned from the Wolford's by early afternoon, and found the cages of chickens under the wagon, the hobbled livestock grazing nearby, and two of our dogs tied to trees. We loaded our rifles and selected vantage points on nearby hillsides from which we could detect any predators.

This was the most important job I had ever been given, and I carefully studied the surrounding hillsides in an attempt to predict where a hungry bear or ferocious cat might appear. A hobbled cow would be easy prey.

I had selected a large tulip poplar to lean against and cut a forked sapling to support the barrel of my muzzleloader. I pondered whether I should try to kill the marauder or just scare it away? Every hide we collected was valuable. They could be tanned for our personal use or traded for powder and lead. I decided that if I had the chance I would shoot to kill.

With food in my stomach and an April sun warming the leafless woods, I became sleepy. I reasoned that I could close my eyes for a few seconds, and never miss anything. I soon fell asleep for nearly an hour. I was pleased to see that all the livestock were still in sight, but disappointed that I was so careless. In spite of my efforts, I dozed on two or three more occasions.

Late afternoon I spotted a dark patch, large enough to be a crouching cat, but not black enough to be a bear. I stared intensely, but could not distinguish a head or a tail. As a large rain cloud darkened the sun, I was positive the object moved. But when the sun returned, I had serious doubts it was a living creature.

If I really was seeing a big cat, I figured it would be better to shoot than to wait for it to make a wild dash downhill at one of the cows. One of my mom's favorite sayings, "Better safe than sorry," came to mind. However, Warner had cautioned me repeatedly about wasting powder and lead.

It would be better to shoot and have it not be a predator, than to not shoot and have it attack our livestock. Although over one hundred yards away, I had no doubt I could hit it. However, I had difficulty holding the forked shooting stick steady and the heavy-barreled muzzleloader would not stop moving side-to-side.

I took a deep breath and prepared to pull the trigger as the rifle barrel once again crossed the target. But before I could shoot, an animal came running through the woods slightly uphill of my intended target. It had a long tail, was tan colored, and the size of a young mountain lion. I quickly swung my rifle barrel to the running animal. Much to my dismay, it began to bark. It was Ulysses! How could I have misidentified a hound dog? My hunting skills still left a lot to be desired.

The unidentified object had not moved, and when Ulysses approached within 10 yards I knew it was not an animal. Dad had told me to always be sure of my target when hunting. He frequently told me, "If you want to see something bad enough, you can convince yourself it is present—even if it is not."

In a few minutes, Dad, Warner, and John returned to our temporary camp. I waited until they were directly across from me and whistled like a bobwhite quail. Warner realized that quail did not live in dense woods and looked in my direction. I slowly waved my hand a couple times and he quickly spotted me. With a smile I stood up and hurried down the hill to join them.

As we sat around a small fire, I revealed my mistaken identity of a mountain lion. Warner responded, "Hunters know it's better to think a stump is a mountain lion, than to think a mountain lion is a stump."

CHAPTER TWELVE

North To Canaan

A light rain soaked the woods during the night but we slept dry beneath the wagon. Bright sunshine greeted us the next morning as we enjoyed bear steaks again.

As Dad, Warner, and John sharpened axes and cross-cut saws our hounds suddenly started barking and ran off toward Red Creek. Within a few minutes we were surprised to hear the jangling of harnesses, followed shortly by the sight of two huge black horses being driven by Ebenezer Flanagan. Caroline and Emma sat atop one black horse, while Lizzie and Daniel rode the other.

After bringing the team to a halt near our wagon, Flanagan explained that he had heard of our troubles and figured it wouldn't hurt to take a day off from planting. He emphasized, "In the wilderness, neighbors help neighbors."

After Flanagan swung his team of Belgians into position Warner and John secured the double trees to the wagon tongue. The draft horses, considerably larger than our team, moved the wagon for several hundred yards. As the grade steepened, they struggled until Flanagan issued the "whoa" command. It was obvious that even the powerful Belgians could not pull our wagon to the summit.

With no other options Dad gave the order to begin unloading. Barrels of flour and cornmeal, boxes of tools, and several pieces of heavy furniture were removed. With the wagon's load reduced, Flanagan snapped the long lead lines against the horse's rumps and they threw their entire weight into the harness. Although straining, the Belgians slowly pulled the wagon up the steep grade. After a couple rest stops the ridge came into view, less than fifty yards away. There was no doubt we would finally see the valley called Canaan.

While Dad, Warner, and John cleared the occasional tree that had fallen across the road, Zedekiah and I eagerly worked our way to the top. We expected to see a great expansive valley before us, but were disappointed to see only a rounded plateau. Our first full view of Canaan Valley must wait until we crossed the plateau.

By late afternoon we had unloaded the half-filled wagon on the summit, returned to get the other half of our belongings, and made a repeat trip. Warner, John, Zedekiah, and I drove our livestock up the steep slope to the summit.

We had no more mountains to climb, only the gentle hillsides of Canaan Valley to traverse. We ate the last of the bear meat for supper, and dropped the bones in a big black kettle to boil. Satisfied that we had conquered the Appalachian Mountains, we slept soundly through the clear, frosty night.

Next morning Caroline removed the bear bones from the kettle, and tossed in several cups of cornmeal and a couple dozen ramps. In a short time, we had broth and the hounds loudly chewed the bones. By mid-morning we had reloaded our belongings. Following an early lunch of bear stew, our horses were harnessed and we were off.

In less than a half mile the land began to slope gently downward and our wagon speed increased. Mac's limp was barely noticeable. Gradually the vista opened and we experienced the magnificence of the southern end of Canaan Valley. Mountain ridges formed the eastern, western, and southern borders, and a prominent ridge extended northward through the valley. That would be the ridge where we planned to establish our homestead. We estimated the valley to be about three miles wide, but we were unable to determine the length.

We crossed a small stream (later named Mill Run) in mid-afternoon and by early evening reached the Freeland homestead. Isaac Freeland and his wife Manera welcomed us, but their two daughters, thirteen-year old Rebecca and eleven-year old Margaret were the most excited. Their mother commented that her daughters had never seen so many good-looking boys in their entire lives. We spent an enjoyable evening with the Freelands, sleeping comfortably in their log barn that night.

After sharing breakfast with the Freelands, our caravan pushed even deeper into Canaan Valley. That night was spent with the Cosners: Solomon and Catherine, and their six children. Also living with them was John Kallogg, a boarder, Almeda Shell, a niece, and their married son, C. C. and his wife, Mary. We learned that only two other families, the Nines and the Easthams, lived in Canaan Valley. The Nine family consisted of John and wife Margaretta, plus seven children. The Eastham family consisted of Robert and his wife, Mary. Their homesteads were located farther west, and we would not pass them due to our land being almost due north.

As we were preparing to depart, Catherine presented Caroline with a small crock and a small cloth bag. Mrs. Cosner commented, "This is a little welcome gift for you. The bag contains buckwheat flour and the crock contains the starter you'll need to prepare the batter. Mix the flour with the starter the night before you plan to fry the buckwheat cakes and by the next morning it will be nice and bubbly, and ready to pour into a hot skillet. The cakes have a pleasant, sour taste and my family likes them better than regular pancakes."

Solomon added, "We haven't had a good corn crop since moving into the valley, due to the short growing season. However, we've been able to grow buckwheat. You won't be able to clear enough land this year to sow buckwheat, but you should plan to grow buckwheat next summer."

As Warner and John hitched Abe and Mack to our wagon, Solomon provided specific directions for us to reach the Sand Run site where we would build our cabin. Although the primitive road ended at the Freeland's homestead, we encountered no major delays.

The massive black cherry trees were widely scattered and the wagon easily rolled between them. Only when we encountered stands of hemlock and red spruce did we need to clear the road.

It occurred to me that forests defined the Allegheny Mountains—not the rugged terrain, and not the rivers, and certainly not the sky. The forests and their diverse tree species are the key to survival in the mountains, for both humans and wildlife.

Before mid-day we had crossed several minor tributaries plus two small streams flowing down off the mountainsides. These would eventually be given the names, Freeland Run and Yoakum Run. Each was less than six feet wide and only a foot or so deep. Fortunately, a brief search never failed to locate a shallow site with low banks where crossing was possible.

By late afternoon we turned westward in search of the ridge that had a north-south orientation. As darkness approached, we reached the sandy, elevated ridge. We camped there for the night, realizing our destination was less than one day away.

With blue sky promising a magnificent spring day, we ate a quick breakfast of dried beef and cold stick break and once again turned Mac and Abe northward. We generally followed the highest portion of the ridge, although Warner and John scouted ahead to locate boggy sites to be avoided.

They learned that the ridge was bordered on the east by a small stream, Sand Run, and on the west by a larger stream, the Blackwater River. The prominent elevated area was about a half mile wide and dominated by monstrous black cherry, the largest we encountered on our entire trip. Most had a girth so great that two people could not reach around them.

Isaac Freeland informed us that Sand Run continued north for about a mile before turning sharply to the west. Upon reaching that landmark we need go no further. By late afternoon, the last week of April, we reached our destination. We halted the horses a few hundred yards short of where the land dropped off sharply to Sand Run.

This would be our last campsite. In a short time a log cabin would rise from the land, followed by a barn, a smokehouse, a chicken coop, and an outhouse—or so we envisioned. Dad asked us to bow our heads and, with Sand Run gurgling not far away, led us in a prayer of thanks that our journey had ended safely.

Chapter Thirteen

The Leatherman Homestead

We had one goal that first exciting day at Sand Run—to find the very best location for our cabin. The site for the cabin and barn should be relatively flat, well-drained, and near a permanent source of drinking water. Ideally the site would face eastward, to catch the morning sun's warming rays. Also, it should be only a short distance from the natural glade that bordered Sand Run. Grassy forage for the livestock was scarce in the forest, but it was plentiful in the glade.

Cosner said that wild grasses in the glade would reach the backs of our cattle by late summer, and provide enough hay to fill our barn and build a dozen large haystacks. We were well aware that without grasses our livestock could not survive the long, harsh winter.

The area overlooking Sand Run was completely forested and in no place did the summer sun reach the forest floor. Huge, towering hardwoods—primarily black cherry and tulip poplar, with an occasional chestnut—dominated. Closer to Sand Run grew dense evergreen stands of hemlock and red spruce.

Following our first breakfast at Sand Run, Dad sent everyone in search of springs. Small seeps were common, but only one large flowing spring was located in the immediate area. It was positioned on the north-facing slope overlooking Sand Run, and based on its depth, water flow, and abundance of moss-covered rocks Dad figured it flowed year-round. Everyone drank freely of the flow exiting from under two large boulders and agreed that it was as sweet as any they had ever tasted, and even colder.

With a large spring as the focal point of our homestead, it was a relatively easy decision where to build the barn, cabin, and outhouse.

We knew none should be uphill of the spring, thus Dad selected sites for the structures where drainage would not contaminate our water source. He designed the cabin to face east, with the front porch providing a vantage point for viewing the morning's sunrise and for watching Sand Run meander through the hemlock-dominated bottomland.

Dad, Warner, and John had assisted with the construction of several log cabins near Short Gap, and were intimately familiar with each step of construction. Rocks must be gathered for the foundation, logs cut for the walls, bark peeled for the roof, and moss collected to fill gaps between logs.

However, before construction started on the cabin, it was necessary to build temporary shelter. We had been warned that May nights in Canaan Valley would be frosty, and hard freezes could occur as late as June.

By sundown of our first full day at Sand Run, we had three large lean-tos. Spruce saplings formed the main supports and slabs of peeled poplar bark provided waterproof roofs. Animal skins and blankets were spread over pungent spruce branches to form beds. The openings of the three shelters faced a single central fire, which was kept burning until the last person fell asleep.

Work began in earnest on the second day. The older boys built a sled of spruce saplings for hauling stones, Dad selected the trees he wanted to cut for the cabin, and Lizzie, Daniel, and I searched for foundation stones. We rolled the small stones to the cabin site and flagged the large ones with spruce branches.

After our mid-day meal, John and Zedekiah hitched Abe to the sled and began hauling stones, while Lizzie, Daniel, and I guided them to our earlier finds. The sounds of double-bitted axes and cross-cut saws filled the cool Canaan air, as Dad and Warner began the Herculean task of dropping the towering poplar trees.

Large stones and small boulders were plentiful and soon Caroline began scrutinizing the outline of the cabin. She complained that it was too small, but Dad explained that the length of available logs determined the size. He promised to build a second room onto the end of the cabin before the first snowfall whitened the valley floor.

Dad estimated we would need at least one hundred logs: forty for the cabin, fifty for the barn, and ten for the small outbuildings. He explained that our biggest problem was finding an adequate number of small logs that could be hauled and hoisted into place to form walls. Most trees growing on the sandy center ridge were too large for cabins or barns, and we had neither the means nor the time to be splitting logs.

After one week, we had completed construction of two, one-hole outhouses, a small chicken coop, a smokehouse, and the stone foundations for our cabin and barn. Dad insisted that we build the small structures first so the older boys could practice cutting notches near the ends of each log, and become comfortable rolling them into place to form walls.

At the end of two weeks, forty logs, mostly tulip poplar, were scattered over the ground near the stone foundation of the cabin, and fifty were resting near the barn site. After the chosen trees had been dropped and cut to desired lengths, Abe and Mac skidded them to the construction sites. Dozens of slabs of peeled poplar bark were spread on the ground and flattened with small logs, to form flat sheets for roofs when dried.

The weather cooperated, with crisp nights and sunny days. A few showers rolled through the valley but caused only minor delays. Work seldom came to a halt. A small clearing, approximately one acre in size, had been created around the cabin site. Sunlight reaching the ground would make it possible to establish a small garden and raise the vegetables that would supplement an otherwise all-meat diet. We had the seeds of cabbage, corn, tomatoes, beans, squash, pumpkins, onions, and turnips to plant around the many stumps.

During the period of felling trees and preparing logs we worked from daylight to dark, with every one of the Leatherman clan busy with assigned chores. Dad and the older boys concentrated on accumulating logs, while Caroline and Lizzie took care of Daniel and little Emma, collected what wild plants were available, and prepared our meals. Ramps were plentiful but were almost too large to enjoy. Fern fiddleheads and a few morels supplemented the ramps. Mostly we ate meat.

We were overjoyed to find that Sand Run was filled with brook trout. Zedekiah and I fished several hours a day and seldom failed to catch enough to feed everyone. Warner and John were the designated hunters and during their scouting trips discovered three shallow spots along Sand Run where deer regularly came to drink.

During the first two weeks they shot three deer and one bear. A deer lasted our family about four days, but a bear lasted a week. What meat was not eaten was salted and dried in our new smokehouse. Likewise, all bear and deer hides were salted, smoked, and saturated with the brains from the dead animal for preservation.

Our hobbled cattle were kept in the glade along Sand Run where succulent new grass shoots were plentiful. Dad was concerned about predators attacking them, and assigned Zedekiah and me to daily guard duty.

Fortunately, we could fish and guard cattle at the same time. I was disappointed that a predator did not show up. Often one or more of our hounds were with us during that time, providing better protection for cattle than Zedekiah or I.

We heard wolves howling several nights and Warner spotted a full-grown mountain lion near Sand Run one evening. It was evident that wolves and lions owned the night and we needed to be extra cautious to prevent the loss of a calf.

One night the first week of May, while we were sitting around the campfire, Lizzie announced, "According to our torn, wrinkled calendar, tomorrow is someone's birthday. I think we should have a little party."

No one answered, as they mentally reviewed the birth dates of each family member. Gradually, they realized that it was my birthday, and smiles came across their faces.

Daniel, only four years old, became excited and shouted, "Yea, a party! I love parties!" Although his birthday coincided with the death day of his mother, we nevertheless had celebrated his fourth birthday with a cake and candles. Daniel asked, "How old will you be, Georgie?"

I proudly answered, "I'll be nine years old."

Lizzie announced, "We must have a cake. We have plenty of

flour and sugar, our cows are giving several gallons of milk and the chickens are laying several eggs each day. What else do you want to eat, Georgie?"

I was a little embarrassed by all the attention, but after a few minutes answered, "I guess hot stick bread and grilled bear ribs would be just fine. The carcass of that big bear John shot is hanging in the smokehouse and we can remove the ribs with our meat saw and grill them over our campfire tomorrow night."

Our cooking stove had been set under an open-sided shelter with poplar bark roof, and when we returned for supper the next evening we were greeted by the scent of fresh-baked cake. Everyone quickly washed up at the trough below the spring and hurried to the campfire.

Dad had cut the ribs so each piece contained two bones. That permitted a long, flexible stick to be inserted between the rib bones and the meat securely held over the fire. With ribs and stick bread slowly browning, our entire family sat around the fire, resting after another demanding day.

As we recounted our day's experiences, Dad pulled a small leather-wrapped item from his pouch. "Here's a little birthday present for you, Georgie."

We seldom received presents, and I was genuinely surprised. Slowly unwrapping the soft deerskin leather, my eyes detected the reflection of polished metal. It was a small hunting knife with a deer-antler handle engraved with the initials, G.S.L. Dad explained that the blacksmith in Romney had made it for him from an old, broken saw blade. He cautioned, "That blade is sharper than any knife you ever used. Be careful that you don't cut off a finger or stab yourself in the leg!"

After everyone had eaten their portions of grilled bear ribs and stick bread, Lizzie brought forth the cake. They asked me to cut it into slices so everyone could have a piece. Counting little Emma, we needed nine pieces. As I clumsily tried to mark the cake into the appropriate number of pieces, Lizzie pronounced, "It's too hard to cut a cake into nine pieces. Why don't you just cut it into eight pieces and we can each share with Emma."

Lizzie led everyone in singing 'Happy Birthday', and in no time the cake was gone. Everyone was in fine spirits as we shared stories about other birthdays. In general, we were all contented. We had enough logs to build our cabin and a barn. The cattle were getting fat and each hen was laying an egg almost every day.

Late May was a marvelous time to live in Canaan Valley. With the coming of warm weather we refreshed our beds of balsam fir branches and washed our blankets in Sand Run.

Our primitive cabin was adequately furnished. The rafters and walls were lined with wooden pegs to hang baskets, firearms, clothing, and cooking utensils. The wall of the front porch was also lined with pegs, and typically held tools, guns, and winter coats. We had constructed a sturdy table and accompanying benches. The table and bench seats were from split poplar logs, while the legs of table and benches were from sections of spruce saplings. We had two similar benches on the front porch—benches that were used daily; to finish a cup of tea after breakfast while watching the sun slowly rise, or to marvel as the glowing rays of a setting sun illuminated the boulders rimming the ridge top. Relaxation was made even more satisfying by the odors of turned earth, burning treetops, and fresh-cut logs.

Caroline did complain almost daily about the floor. She had been spoiled by having a board floor in our house in the South Branch Valley, and never accepted the dirt floor in our Canaan cabin. Once the spring rains had diminished, the floor was almost always dry. A sweeping with a broom of spruce branches removed most leaves or other debris that had been brought inside when one of the boys did not wipe off his boots. I thought the floor was almost clean enough to eat off of, which Emma and the hounds did on more than one occasion.

Finally, in response to Caroline's complaining, Dad promised, "I'll build you a solid floor after we build a pit and accompanying platform to saw logs into boards. However, we must build a small barn and must begin harvesting the marsh hay in a couple weeks. In the meantime, the slabs of poplar bark left over from roofing the cabin and barn will make a decent floor."

The slabs were each two to three feet wide and nearly six feet long. They were placed with the outer side down and the cream-colored side facing up. One problem with a dirt floor is you cannot find small things that you drop, especially the dark colored ones. The light-colored bark made it possible to find small objects without crawling around on our hands and knees while holding a flaming candle. With the table, benches, and beds holding them in place the bark slabs made a nice floor. Or at least I thought so.

Caroline reluctantly acknowledged, "This bark floor is better than dirt. However, we need a smooth board floor, and a real wooden door. The old piece of canvas we use now for a door won't keep out the cold. Also, we need to chink between the logs before cold weather arrives. The cracks let in fresh air now, but in a few months we will be concerned about keeping the outside air out."

CHAPTER FOURTEEN

Predators

One evening in early June, after Dad finished the blessing, and while a large pot of venison stew was being passed around the table, Zedekiah commented, "There're many wonderful things about Canaan, but there's one we should be especially thankful for. There are no poisonous snakes. Actually, there are few snakes of any kind. We've seen four or five water snakes along Sand Run, a few green snakes in the marsh grass, and a couple small snakes with yellow rings around their necks under the trunks of fallen trees. But no rattlesnakes or copperheads!"

Warner added, while staring directly at me, "Also, we haven't seen a single puffing adder. That must disappoint some people." I tried to maintain a straight face, while Lizzie frowned. Caroline had quite a scowl on her face.

To change the subject, I quickly added, "There's an even more special thing about this amazing valley. There's no poison ivy! I can go barefooted, or carry armloads of fresh cut hay, or roll in the grass as much as I want without worrying about breaking out in dreaded itchy blisters."

Zedekiah added to our list of blessings by noting, "The hounds are also happy. They have plenty of animals to chase and haven't had a single tick since we settled here. A hound without ticks must think it lives in heaven."

John noted, "It's wonderful there are no poisonous snakes, or ticks, or poison ivy. But not so rewarding to have no bullfrogs. Canaan has only those little green frogs. Their legs aren't much bigger than a chipmunk's, way too small to eat. I do miss those huge bullfrogs that lived along the South Branch, and the big, juicy frog legs we used to fry in the skillet."

Of more immediate blessings, Zedekiah had located several serviceberry trees growing in the wood's edge where the forest met the marsh on both sides of Sand Run. These small trees, fifteen to twenty feet tall, were hanging heavy with reddish-purple fruits that resembled small apples. We ate these by the dozens, crunching their small almond-flavored seeds before swallowing a mouth full.

After filling several baskets with the low-hanging fruits, we stood on the horses backs to reach those higher up. Warner, John, and Zedekiah picked most of them because they were the tallest.

We couldn't climb the slender trees because they weren't strong enough to support our weight. I wanted to help, but they were concerned I might fall and hit my head. Lizzie constantly reminded me of the warning that another blow to the head could prove fatal.

As we ate serviceberry biscuits and deer stew, followed by serviceberry cobbler, everyone was in a thoughtful mood. It appeared that Canaan would indeed be the promised land we had anticipated.

But Canaan presented a slew of problems we had not faced in the Potomac Valley, not the least of which were predators. The lives of our chickens, cattle, and even the hounds were at risk. Rarely a week went by when we didn't spot two or three black bears rambling through the woods. Mountain lions were present, but rarely seen. Their frightening screams jerked us from deep sleep on many a night, but we had actually spotted only five during daylight hours.

Bobcats roamed throughout the forests and marshes, as did gray foxes and raccoons. By July we had spotted several dozen of these mid-sized predators. They didn't pose a danger to us, but they could have easily killed our chickens. We were much surprised, and disappointed, not to see red foxes, which were so abundant in the Potomac Valley.

The howls of a timber wolf were also heard, but seemed much less threatening than did those of a mountain lion—possibly because they were not too different from the howl of a hound dog. We had heard that every major drainage in the Cheat Mountains supported a pack of wolves during the late 1700s, when buffalo, elk, and white-tailed deer were present. However, by the mid-1800s it became evident that the mountains would not support both wolves and settlers.

Directly and indirectly, settlers were responsible for the elimination of timber wolves. We had learned in school that by 1825, the last buffalo in West Virginia had been shot, thus eliminating one important food source for wolves. By the 1850s only a few scattered elk roamed the mountain valleys and white-tailed deer numbers were so low the wolves were forced to turn to other food sources. Rabbits, wild turkeys, and beaver are acceptable foods to wolves, but a pack cannot survive on small game alone.

Dad explained to us how timber wolves were indeed shot, and trapped, and poisoned. The wolves did kill a few sheep and calves when their natural food supplies dwindled. But Dad concluded it was the perceived threat rather than the real threat that led to their demise at human hands. Settlers depended on livestock to feed their families, and any threat to their domestic animals' survival must be eliminated. Steel traps and rifles accounted for the deaths of hundreds of wolves, as ever more land was cleared and more farms were established.

I vividly remember my grandfather talking about bounties being paid as early as 1788—to expedite the wolves' extermination from the Cheat Mountains. The bounty on a full-grown wolf was only $3.33 in 1801, but had risen to $25.00 by 1880 when we arrived. Randolph County paid bounties on more than fifty wolves annually during the early 1800s.

Cosner explained to Dad that scalps of wolves killed in the Dry Fork drainage found their way to the Randolph County courthouse in Elkins where the bounty was eagerly paid. Officials cared little where the wolf was killed, believing the only good wolf was a dead wolf.

Warner and John were overjoyed the first time they heard a wolf howl. They talked confidently about killing it and collecting the bounty. All agreed this would be our best opportunity to obtain cash money. Zedekiah and I were equally confident, and frequently discussed what we would buy with our bounty money.

One other mid-sized predator, a fisher, inhabited the Sand Run watershed. This unusual mammal was slightly larger than a gray fox, which it closely resembled when seen from a distance. Most people called it a black fox because its fur was brownish black rather than orange-gray like that of the gray fox. They both had long, bushy tails. Capable of climbing trees, this ten-pound member of the weasel family was a true carnivore. Their prey included rabbits, red squirrels, mice, grouse, wild turkey, and deer fawns. Anything they could catch was a potential meal.

Weasels harassed our chicken several nights in May and June, and managed to kill one old hen before we trapped two of them in steel traps. We were concerned about the safety of a Rhode Island Red hen that had a clutch of ten eggs alongside the barn. If they hatched and survived we could look forward to many more eggs in the skillet in the years to come. That particular hen, named Biddy, had been hand-raised by Lizzie from the day it emerged from the egg.

One night in June, we were all awakened by a terrible ruckus in the chicken house. With a quarterly moon barely illuminating the scene, we all gathered on the front porch. All four of us boys grabbed our rifles while Dad lit a spruce knot with a glowing coal from the fireplace. Lizzie called dramatically, "Oh please, protect Biddy from the killer."

By the time we finished pulling on our pants and boots the hounds had crossed Middle Ridge and were headed for the Blackwater River. We followed in pursuit.

I loved the excitement! Unable to see much except the flaring spruce knot and a few huge tree trunks, one's imagination dominates. Your mind creates scenes to compensate for the failure of your eyesight—scenes more detailed and more dramatic than ever possible during daylight. In a few minutes, my mind had created bobcats, and black bears, and mountain lions, and timber wolves, all waiting to spring upon us from the safety of darkness.

In less than ten minutes we caught up with the hounds. I was confident we were beneath a snarling mountain lion, or possibly even two of them. If they sprang from the tree, one of us would certainly be seriously injured, if not killed. We wouldn't be able to shoot for fear of hitting one another.

Dad circled the huge sugar maple while my brothers and I spread out around its trunk. At first we could see nothing. I figured there could be five or ten black bears in the tree and we could never see them in the darkness. But John told us, "Look for its eyes, they'll be reflected by the flame."

Dad continued to circle the tree trunk while we moved our heads back and forth, and up and down. After a minute or so Zedekiah called excitedly, "I see it! I see its eyes!" We all quickly gathered behind him, while John lit another spruce knot. Now we all saw the pair of greenish-yellow eyes, blinking on and off similar to a pair of stars in the night sky.

John offered, "I think it's a bobcat, or possibly a young mountain lion."

Warner suggested, "I think it's a bear, but there's only one way to find out."

Zedekiah leaned his rifle barrel firmly alongside a nearby black cherry, and with Warner holding a small flaming spruce limb to illuminate the sights Zedekiah drew a careful bead. At the sound of the gunpowder exploding, the eyes stopped glowing.

Much to my disappointment it was too small to be a bear or a mountain lion. As it landed among the snarling dogs it appeared black—not gray like a raccoon, or tan like a bobcat. Warner and John pulled the hounds away and tied them to a nearby tree, while we examined the strange mammal.

In the light of the flames we could see its coat and long bushy tail were glossy brown, not black. Sharp canine teeth identified it as a carnivore. We all agreed it was a fisher. Gathering the hounds we began our walk back to the cabin, confident there was one less predator to prey upon our chickens.

CHAPTER FIFTEEN

The Census Taker

W e received our first human visitor on June 1. That particular morning, we were working to complete the two-story barn. The sturdy log walls had been completed in May and we were adding the individual stalls for the horses and cows and the floor for the hayloft. Suddenly the dogs began barking loudly. We dropped our tools, ready to jump down and grab our rifles. But upon hearing the tinkling of bells we relaxed.

This was a special treat, regardless of who our visitor might be. A horseman came into view, and appeared to be about thirty years old, deeply tanned, and wore a white cotton shirt, heavy leather boots, and black broad-brimmed hat. His brown mare's saddle had bells hanging from the rear. Dad walked out to meet him, and said, "Greetings stranger. What brings you out here in this wilderness?"

Dismounting, the man answered, "I'm Stuard Lambert, the census taker. And I'm visiting every house in Canaan and the Dry Fork District of Tucker County to record information about each person. The government hopes to count everyone in the United States and document the numbers in each of the thirty-eight states. This is the first day of the census and I must have my work done by July 1st, the deadline set by the government."

Dad commented, "I lived in Hampshire County during the 1870 census and remember a man from the government visiting our house. I guess you want the same information. We're about ready to take a break. Why don't you join us and we can provide all the information you need after eating."

Dad continued, "Georgie, take Mr. Lambert's horse and tie it in the shade under the big sugar maple tree. Be certain it can reach lots of green grass."

After everyone washed at the spring, we relaxed on the front porch with cold biscuits left over from breakfast. Lizzie passed butter and honey, and brought out cups of buttermilk, offering the first one to Mr. Lambert.

He said, "I'd rather drink cool buttermilk than anything else I can think of on a warm summer day."

As we finished the biscuits, Dad asked, "What's going on in the outside world? We haven't heard any news since April, when we left Mineral County."

Lambert repeated the news he had already given to the Cosners. "Reconstruction from the Civil War is still going slowly, but there seems to be some progress. Rutherford Hayes is still the President, and seems to be doing a better job than did Grant. Most people think Hayes will be re-elected.

Newspapers reported they've started digging the Panama Canal, and Wabash, Indiana, has the first electric streetlights in the entire country. The paper reported they have electric streetlights throughout the whole town. That Edison fellow might change the whole world."

We had seen a picture of a light bulb in the newspaper before we left Mineral County, but none of us could imagine them lighting an entire town.

After the break, Lambert opened a leather satchel, pulled out a printed sheet of paper, and began asking Dad questions.

"Mr. Leatherman, I need to know the names of everyone who lives here and their ages as of June 1. Let's start with your full name and exact age."

Dad answered, "George W. Leatherman, forty-four years old."

"Now, your wife and children," Lambert requested.

Dad continued, "My wife is Caroline Thrush Leatherman, thirty-one years old. Sons are Warner W., age twenty, John W., eighteen, Zedekiah, thirteen, George S., nine, and Daniel R., four. I have two daughters, Mary E., age eleven, and Emma M. age two."

After carefully writing down all the information in the proper little blocks on his printed paper, Stuard Lambert asked, "What's your occupation?"

Dad answered, "I guess you can list me as a farmer, although I did considerable preaching when we lived in Mineral County."

Lambert continued, "I need to know the state where everyone was born and whether they're white, black, mulatto, or Chinese."

"Caroline, Warner, and I were born in what was then Virginia, but now is West Virginia."

Lambert interjected, "I've been told to record your birthplace as Virginia, in that case. What about the others?"

Dad added, "John was born in Indiana, and the others were all born in West Virginia. We're all white, as you can readily see."

Lambert continued, "Have any of your children gone to school this year, and which ones cannot read or write?"

"None of the children have gone to school this year. Daniel and Emma cannot read or write. Little George can write his name and a few words. He can read most short words, but has difficulty reading books. Mary Elizabeth can write her name and several words. In addition, she can read most common words and short verses in the Bible."

Lambert asked one other question, "Do you know of any other families beyond here in Canaan Valley?

Dad responded, "As far as we know there are no others. My boys have explored most of this valley, and haven't seen another cabin— other than the Cosners, Freelands, Easthams, and Nines. Warner calls the land to the north of us that great un-peopled land."

The visitor said, "The tax man at the Tucker County Courthouse in St. George estimated there are ninety families living in the Dry Fork District and I need to be off. I want to spend the night in the Nine's barn before heading farther south."

I had wanted to ask how much he was paid to do the census work, how many families he would visit, how many wild animals he had seen, and a whole host of other questions. But I remained quiet, having been taught that youngsters should be seen and not heard.

Dad firmly declared, "Let's get back to the barn. We've wasted enough time today."

CHAPTER SIXTEEN

Hay Stacks

The dense marsh grasses were ready to be harvested by the first week of July. We spent one whole day sharpening our scythes, sanding the long curved handles, and making sure all parts were secure. We repaired the sled and built five new pitchforks from split poplar saplings, two with four tines and three with only three tines.

We erected the center poles for five haystacks. Each spruce pole, twelve inches wide at the base and nearly twenty-five feet tall, was set three feet into the ground and braced with rocks. A platform of smaller poles flush on the ground would elevate the hay enough to prevent rotting of the bottom layer.

With the five of us men, more accurately three men and two boys, spread out in a line across one end of a stand of marsh grass, our hay harvest began. The steady, rhythmic swinging of a scythe and cradle is strenuous, although rewarding. You have only to glance behind you to see the trailing swath of flattened green grass showing your progress for the day. In less than an hour sweat had soaked our shirts and was threatening to do the same to our pants.

By mid-morning we had cut nearly an acre and Dad called for our first rest. We trudged to a few boulders along Sand Run, removed our wet shirts and broad-rimmed hats, and dipped them in the cool water.

Zedekiah wistfully said, "I sure wish we had a swimming hole like we did on Patterson Creek. I'd jump in, clothes and all."

John answered, "If you weren't such a sissy you'd jump in Sand Run."

With a scowl Zedekiah said, "If you're so tough why don't you do it."

We all grinned. We had tried earlier in July to take a dip in Sand Run, and concluded the swift-flowing stream must never get warm enough for swimming.

At noon Caroline, Lizzie, Daniel, and little Emma brought baskets filled with cold meat and biscuits. While we dived into the baskets, Lizzie and Daniel lugged jugs of drinking water from Sand Run. Lizzie, Daniel, and Emma began hunting for crawdads and water snakes in the creek while Dad, my brothers, and I took short naps. It was almost like a picnic.

Work continued through the hot afternoon till evening when Dad announced, "It's quitting time boys. We've cut nearly five acres and need to save some for tomorrow."

Wearily, we trudged home. As we plopped onto the porch, Dad hollered, "Caroline, you better bring our supper out onto the porch. We're too tired to come in."

We cut marsh grasses for two more days and then began hauling sleds full of the dried grasses to the set spruce poles. Dad and Warner stacked the hay neatly around the pole while the rest of us steadily pitched clumps of grass up to them. In less than two hours Dad and Warner slid off the top of one pear-shaped stack and we stood back to admire their work.

John noted, "It's leaning a little towards the mountain, but I guess it'll still be standing when the snow flies."

The smell of dried grasses always reminded me of those nights I had slept in a barn—a scent so earthy, so invigorating, and so satisfying. I wondered if cattle were equally affected by the scent, or more so because it involved their sense of taste.

Our good fortune held, and July days remained hot and dry. By the end of the sixth day the bottomland along Sand Run was graced with five impressive haystacks and the small barn was half-filled.

On the Sabbath, Dad conducted church services for most of the morning. He read verses from his Bible and Caroline sang a few hymns. Each of the Leatherman children, even Warner, was expected to recite a new Bible verse each week. I usually chose a verse involving animals.

After our day of rest we began swinging the scythes through another stand of tough marsh grass. Unfortunately, a hard rain fell the second night and soaked the nearly three acres of hay we had cut. Pitchforks replaced scythes and we spent the rest of the next day lifting and turning the hay so it would dry properly. Wet grass will mildew and rot.

After we had dried the hay, we used our sled to haul it across the small bridge we had constructed over Sand Run, and continued to fill the barn. This is where we would keep the milk cows during those winter months when the snow was too deep for them to graze outside.

With the hay harvested, Dad gave us a much-deserved break and suggested we explore the three main streams that flowed nearby. John and Warner were assigned the Blackwater River. Zedekiah worked his way up and down Glade Run, while I followed Sand Run to its headwaters, passing through several dense stands of hemlock along the way.

I discovered that Sand Run originated at a very unusual spring flowing steadily from the mountainside. Much of the water seeped out of the ground from under boulders, but in one small, clear pool a short distance from the boulders, the water silently vented from a prominent hole in the bottom of the stream. Swirling sand around the hole was the most obvious sign that water was gushing from underground, but from where I had no idea. My guess was that it had to be coming from the mountain to the east, flowing underground through layers of sandstone before emerging at the headwaters of Sand Run.

Much to my surprise, Zedekiah reported similar roiling springs erupting from the bottom of Glade Run at two different sites. Neither John nor Warner detected similar oddities, possibly because the Blackwater River was wider and deeper than both Glade Run and Sand Run.

We carried fishing poles and always returned with enough fish for dinner. I was amazed to see dozens of large brook trout drifting lazily in the cold, shallow headwaters of Sand Run, almost all facing upstream in anticipation of an insect or worm floating by. After several dozen fishing trips we concluded that Canaan Valley had no bass and no catfish, only brook trout. We all loved the pink-fleshed brook trout, but missed the battles we had experienced with jumping smallmouth bass in Patterson Creek.

By late July our beans, squash, potatoes, cabbage, and corn seedlings were looking good. Dad was confident our root cellar would be well stocked come October. I had discovered a small stand of chestnut trees east of Sand Run and we anticipated harvesting dozens of burlap sacks full of the sweet, rich nuts when they dropped in October.

Chapter Seventeen
Cabin Mountain

In August we suffered a serious loss. One foggy morning, Warner discovered the bloody carcass of one of our Jersey calves in a hemlock stand. The calf had been partially eaten, and then covered with grass and small branches. It was obvious a mountain lion had been the culprit. Warner and John immediately gathered the hounds, rifles, extra food and blankets and set out in pursuit of the big cat. Dad encouraged them as they departed, "Do your best to kill the varmint, even if it takes a week. We can't afford to lose any more livestock."

Eight days later, my brothers returned. Warner reported, "We followed that cat's trail all the way up onto the plateau that forms the eastern border of Canaan Valley, where it apparently entered one of the many large piles of boulders. The hounds howled and barked at one large opening, but wouldn't go into the hole. I didn't blame them. We built a fire at the opening and kept it burning for two days but don't know if we killed the cat."

John added, "We did some exploring and made some important discoveries. That plateau (which would later be known as Dolly Sods) is covered with blueberries. Cosner told us some Confederate scouts camped there during the Civil War and their campfire escaped, burning hundreds of acres. Those burned sites grew back in blueberries—solid stands of dense blueberries. We must have picked ten gallons while we were up there."

"Also, the blueberry patches are criss-crossed with animal trails. Most appear to have been made by rabbits. We saw several of the rabbits and I shot two. They're bigger than the cottontails we hunted along the South Branch, and have much larger hind feet."

Dad answered, "Isaac Freeland told us about the large rabbits that live up on the plateau. Hares, he called them."

John responded, "Rabbits or hares, they're sure good to eat. I wish they lived down here on the valley floor."

Warner explained how they had discovered a small, dilapidated cabin of spruce logs, large enough to accommodate two people.

Dad said, "Freeland told us about a cabin on the mountain that had been built by Confederate scouts during the Civil War. That must be the one he was referring to."

John added, "I sure wish those soldiers had built a chimney. They left a small opening in the roof, so smoke could escape from any fires built on the cabin floor, but no chimney. Warner and I plan to spend a couple weeks up there after cold weather arrives, hunting and trapping. If we have any spare time we'll add a small fireplace and chimney."

While my brothers were in pursuit of the mountain lion, I hunted almost every morning. I still had not killed a bear or a deer, but did manage to bring down one young turkey. It had flown up into a hemlock when it detected me sneaking through the woods. I spotted its outline and was able to get a solid rest for my muzzleloader. I made a good shot. Lizzie told me what a great hunter I was that evening as we ate fried turkey.

Hunting in Canaan Valley I had little risk of getting lost. I became confused a couple times, but the Canaan topography was so accommodating I always got back. Both the mountain along the eastern side of Canaan Valley and the sand ridge where our cabin was situated ran north-south. Glade Run flowed south to north then turned westward before joining the Blackwater, which flowed in a northerly direction. Sand Run ran south to north for most of its length.

Much to our surprise—and deep regret—we had discovered there were no oak trees in Canaan Valley, and thus, no gray squirrels. We found a few small red squirrels in the spruce stands, but those fairy diddles, as we called them, were too small to eat. Besides, they tasted like turpentine when cooked. Without gray squirrels, rabbits, or groundhogs I didn't have many small animals to hunt. Although I hunted a couple hours each day I usually came home empty-handed.

I was never able to stalk within range of a deer to get a decent shot. On three occasions I fired my muzzleloader at one, but each time I missed. I never had a shot at a bear although I saw one almost every week.

Warner convinced me I would be successful in the fall, when deer and bear concentrated near chestnut and beech trees. Nevertheless, my failure to kill a large animal dampened my dreams of becoming the best hunter in my family. If they depended on me to put meat on the table they would surely go hungry.

One night, as Lizzie was working with Daniel on his numbers she commented, "I think I'd like to be a teacher when I'm older. I enjoy helping youngsters with their reading and their numbers. I think I did a pretty good job with you, Little Georgie. You can do your multiplication tables up through tens and can write many common words."

I was lying on the cabin floor, trying to read about Noah and the flood in the Bible, and nodded my head but didn't say anything. I liked Lizzie better than any of my other brothers and sisters, but I really didn't like her to call me "Little Georgie." I was almost ten years old!"

Lizzie asked, "What do you want to be when you grow up, Little Georgie?"

I thought for a moment, because it wasn't something I had ever given much thought, and, after several minutes, answered, "I want to be a great hunter, and provide our family with all the meat they can eat."

Lizzie answered, "I'm certain with a little experience you'll be bringing home a bear or a deer every week."

After more thought, I added, "When I'm older I'd like to write stories, but I don't think I could ever write books like Mark Twain. His story about the adventures of Tom Sawyer was special. You know I'm not that good with my sentences. Besides, I don't have anything to write about."

Zedekiah interjected, "Maybe you could write a book about Angus McCallander, the Scotsman Grandpa Leatherman used to talk about. Someone certainly needs to write a book about that amazing man who traveled through the Appalachian wilderness with a tame wolf in the 1750s."

Lizzie noted, "You might even have a story written about your own life—a biography they call it."

I answered, "I haven't done anything exciting like Angus McCallander. I've never lived with the Indians, or built a dugout canoe, or raised a wolf pup, or traveled alone into the wilderness, or saved someone's life."

Lizzie responded, "That's not true, Georgie. You've done lots of exciting things that boys in big cities never even dream about doing. You raised a crow, fell out of a tree while trying to catch a hawk, trapped fur animals, and came into a wilderness that's just as dangerous as the country where Angus lived. You even killed a wild turkey with a muzzleloader, just like Angus."

Zedekiah interjected, "Heck, you were a real cowboy when only six years old and did something that Angus never did. You rode a cow! You could write about that."

I frowned, but said nothing. I would have been embarrassed if my whole family had seen me riding Belle when Lizzie and I ran away.

Lizzie ended the conversation before returning to her lessons with Daniel, "Everyone's life is an adventure when read and relived by people 100 years after it happens. They can experience the wilderness much as you are now, the abundant brook trout, the towering black cherry trees, the wolves, the joys, and the disappointments. You should start writing down your adventures in a journal. That would help you remember the details of your life."

CHAPTER EIGHTEEN

Autumn Glory

B y August we were picking green beans, yellow squash, and carrots almost every day. Although tomatoes had not yet ripened, dozens of green ones were hanging from the vines. The corn was nearly four feet tall, but still had small ears. Heads of cabbage and hills of potatoes were maturing and we anticipated harvesting several bushels in September.

Dad was quite optimistic that we would harvest a surplus of garden produce, and would need a place to store it when temperatures dropped below freezing. Thus, he directed the construction of a root cellar on the hillside near the cabin. The completed cellar was six feet wide and six feet deep, and extended eight feet back into the hillside. The top was covered with logs, then large strips of bark, and eventually with a one-foot layer of soil. The front was made of logs, with a small log door suspended with leather straps.

Our plans for a bountiful harvest were dampened the first week of September. We had built a small warming fire in the fireplace one night and brought out thin blankets to take off the chill. We woke the next morning to find a silvery white coating of frost over the fields and garden. Although pretty to look at, we knew the garden would suffer. By afternoon, the green leaves of beans, squash, and tomatoes had blackened, and we knew their growing season had come to a sudden halt.

Dad lamented as we sat on the porch, "I was warned the growing season wouldn't extend far into September in some years, but I'd hoped we could get a good garden harvest our first summer here in Canaan. The heads of cabbage can withstand a frost but the potatoes most likely won't attain full size. Ears of corn will never mature and our root cellar will be empty before the New Year arrives."

Temperatures rose that afternoon, offering a faint glimmer of hope, but frosts appeared six more times in early September and our water buckets were decorated with ice three consecutive mornings the second week of September.

The arrival of bright foliage colors confirmed the beginning of another season. Almost daily, Lizzie commented on the glory of autumn. I remember her stating, "I wish I had a coat that matched the many colors of the Canaan hillsides. The quiet, soft blend of yellows, reds, oranges, browns, and greens would produce a beautiful coat, or dress for that matter."

With little to do about the garden crisis, my brothers and I concentrated our efforts on hunting and gathering nuts. During late September and early October, we hunted most mornings and spent afternoons searching for chestnut trees or fishing for brook trout. By mid-October several baskets of sweet chestnuts had been stored in the root cellar and sweet-smelling hardwood smoke drifted slowly from cracks in the smokehouse.

Dad encouraged us to accumulate even more dried trout, venison, and bear. Fortunately, bears were more abundant than deer, and easier to hunt—especially when they were feeding under chestnut trees. Bears were more desirable than deer because of the thick layer of fat that built up under their hides prior to hibernation. The thick chunks of fat were melted in a large kettle over a small fire then processed into lard and candles. Without lard there would be no baking, and without candles the only light in our cabin would be reflected from the fireplace.

With our smokehouse nearly overflowing I didn't think we would run out of meat, but Dad warned us about the difficulties of hunting and trapping with large winter snows. "By January, the drifts will be so high you boys won't be able to see over them. Besides, you'll be busy feeding our livestock and maintaining paths to and from the barn."

One day in late October I experienced a huge thrill while scouting along Sand Run for tracks. As I examined the carcass of a buck that had been killed and partially buried by a mountain lion, I spotted a wolf slinking along the edge of a spruce thicket. After emerging from behind the trunk of a large spruce, and clearly in view, it stopped to urinate. When it crouched, I realized it was a female. Suddenly the wolf turned and stared directly at me. Mesmerized, I felt no urge to raise my muzzleloader. After two or three minutes the wolf turned and faded into the spruce.

At supper that night, I reported my discovery. Enthusiastically, I proposed, "Since it's a female, she could have pups next spring. I'd give anything to have a wolf pup for a pet like the one Granddad Leatherman told us about that the Scotsman had trained. It followed obediently at his side, and even helped him hunt deer and bears?"

All summer my brothers and I had schemed and planned how we would kill a wolf and collect the bounty. I had even selected the new carbine gun I would buy with the bounty money. But now my goal wavered. Rather than killing the wolf, I envisioned capturing one of its pups, and raising it to be my constant companion. All we needed to do was find its den next spring, and dig out the pups. After I had trained my wolf to hunt, the two of us would bring home dozens, possibly even hundreds of deer and bear hides. Their value would greatly exceed the bounty the wolf's scalp would bring.

Although we were tempted to relax during the warm autumn afternoons, we tried to locate another crop of the mountains—ginseng plants. The dried roots, in great demand in Oriental countries, would supplement our furs when we traded for needed supplies in Parsons. Everyone other than Caroline and little Emma searched for the ginseng. We'd spend an entire day searching for the red-berried plant. We would rejoin for lunch when Dad blew the cow horn he carried. On two occasions, I found a thick patch of the plant and collected considerably more than anyone else. I was really proud when Lizzie bragged on me.

Zedekiah was hunting ginseng alone, one overcast September day, along the lower flank of Cabin Mountain, overlooking Glade Run, when he spotted something none of us had even seen. As he reported after returning home that evening, "You'll never believe what I saw today. I first thought it was a deer, but it was nearly twice the size of a typical white-tailed doe. It had antlers, but they didn't fork like a buck's. There was one main beam with small branches coming off the side, but the antlers seemed to extend backwards rather than forward. The animal was feeding on the opposite side of Glade Run, among clumps of dried marsh grasses. It was dark brown, with a light-colored rump. I tried to get close enough for a shot, but it must have heard me trying to cross Glade Run and it took off up over the Middle Ridge. It didn't jump like a deer, but ran stiff-legged. Sort of like one of those horses we saw at the harness races in Romney last summer. I'm convinced it was an elk. Although I never saw one I did see pictures in some of our old school books."

Dad added, "Isaac Freeland told us that elk were last seen in Canaan Valley during the Civil War, although he was certain he had seen their tracks in the valley on two or three occasions. Someone in Parsons told him elk tracks were spotted at the headwaters of the Cheat River in 1873."

Warner, John, and I got quite excited about shooting an elk. We didn't know what their meat would taste like, but figured it was just as good as venison. We spent the next two days hunting the Middle Ridge, but never caught another glimpse of the animal.

Another vivid memory I have of that summer of 1880 was the small ceremony we held on the fifth anniversary of my Mother's death. After supper we gathered on the porch and Lizzie recited the words she had memorized in school four years earlier. Her recitation was halted several times as she wiped away tears. I noticed, while quietly crying myself, that everyone else in the family, other than Caroline, was also wiping tears.

There's one sweet little treasure, that I'll ever dearly prize,
better far, than all the wealth beneath the wave.
I've a small faded floret that I plucked in childhood days,
tis a flower from my angel mother's grave.
In the quiet country churchyard they laid her down to sleep,
close beside the old home she's at rest.

And the low sacred mound is enshrined within my heart,
by the sweet ties of love forever blest.
Treasured in my memory, like a happy dream,
are the loving words she gave.
But my heart still fondly clings to the dry and withered leaves,
tis a flower from my angel mother's grave.
In the still and silent night, I often dream of home,
and the vision tells me ever to be brave.
But the one link that binds me to that place I love so well,
tis the flower from my angel mother's grave.

CHAPTER NINETEEN

A Successful Hunt

My failure as a big-game hunter finally ended in late October. I was hunting along the Blackwater River. Rain clouds scudded slowly eastward, while sporadic breezes drove the low-hanging fog first one direction then another. Upturned leaves on the maples foretold an afternoon shower.

While leaning against a hemlock, I spotted a white, twitching tail at the edge of an alder thicket not far from the river. When the feeding animal raised its head to search for danger, I identified it as a small buck.

A small sugar maple sapling provided a rest for my muzzleloader and I set the front sight slightly behind the animal's shoulder, just as Warner had taught me. When the deer stepped into a small opening, providing a clear shot, I slowly squeezed the trigger. In the excitement, I forgot to hold the stock firmly against my shoulder and received a stiff wallop. As the smoke cleared and I recovered from the jolt I searched for the deer. But it was nowhere to be seen. I heard it running in the alders and knew I had not hit it solidly. I nervously reloaded my muzzleloader with fresh powder, wadding, and a shiny lead ball and sat down to wait.

After pausing five or ten minutes, as I had been taught, I began a cautious search. I had no trouble finding where the deer was standing when I shot, and saw a spot of fresh blood in the grass. Suddenly I detected it out of the corner of my eye! My very first deer lay dead not ten yards away. The antlers weren't huge, and the body was only mid-sized. I figured it was only two or three years old. I loudly exclaimed, "Yes, Yes, Yes!"

Carefully leaning my rifle against a tree, I pulled out my hunting knife and began the butchering process. After making a long careful slit the length of the belly, I reached inside the cavity to make the cuts necessary to release the steaming innards. The stomach spilled out and I extended the knife into the chest cavity to sever the heart and the lungs. Working entirely by feel, I had difficulty making the proper cuts. Finally though, the heart came loose and I was able to pull the lungs from the cavity. With the innards removed, the carcass would begin to cool.

I wiped my hands and knife in dried grass then rolled the animal onto its belly so blood would flow out onto the ground. After rolling the carcass I noticed my hands were bloody. With more dried grass I again wiped them clean. Much to my surprise, a few minutes later I noticed that one was still bloody. A close examination revealed a clean cut running across the palm of my left hand.

Apparently, while holding the heart with my left hand and severing the heart's connections with the right hand, I had managed to slice open my palm. Pain didn't appear until I was washing my hands. The cold water caused sharp stinging, but the cut was not dangerously deep. I held a large clump of green moss firmly against the cut. The wound continued to bleed for only a few minutes before I collected another clump of moss and grasped it firmly inside my fist.

Gathering my rifle, and putting the deer heart in my hunting pouch, I joyously headed up the hillside toward our cabin. There was no way I could pull the dead buck up the hillside and didn't even want to try with my cut hand.

The sun had disappeared behind the trees surrounding our cabin as I strode up the front steps. John, Zedekiah, and Daniel were sitting on the front porch, watching the slow-moving clouds. Dad and Warner had taken our ginseng roots to Parsons to trade for sacks of flour and cornmeal. Caroline and Lizzie were inside fixing supper, while Emma played on the bark floor.

Walking past those on the porch I stuck my head into the cabin and announced, "Does anyone want to see what I have?"

Lizzie answered, "Sure, you know I do."

After Lizzie and Caroline wiped their hands they came outside. I ceremoniously opened my hunting pouch, and I revealed the bright red heart.

With a big grin on my face, I asked, "What do you think of that?"

Everyone immediately began to talk at once. I distinctly remember Lizzie saying, "You're a real hunter now! Someday, you'll be the best hunter in Canaan Valley!"

John and Zedekiah brought Abe from the barn and I led them to the deer carcass. As darkness settled, Abe trudged into the barn with my buck tied across his back. After hanging the buck from a barn beam to drain and cool we sat down to a supper of fried deer liver.

Lizzie noticed the clump of moss I held in my left hand and asked, "What are you holding that moss for? Is it good luck or something?

I said, "Oh, I hurt my hand a little bit."

Lizzie sternly ordered, "Let me see. I'll take care of it."

I opened my hand and let the moss drop onto the bark floor. Lizzie gasped, "Oh no! It looks like you cut yourself clear to the bone. What happened?"

While I detailed my adventure, Lizzie brought some dried moss from a basket hanging from a rafter. She pressed it firmly against the cut, which was oozing blood from one corner, and ordered, "Hold this against the cut. Dried moss is much better than green moss to stop bleeding and to stop infection."

Caroline emphatically noted, "You need to keep it clean and apply a poultice of goldenseal. If you don't, you'll get gangrene and your whole arm will rot off."

Then she added, "I remember your Dad telling you when you got that knife that you had to be careful. It was so sharp you could cut off your hand. Now it appears that you almost did."

I answered, "Aw, it's only a little cut. I'm not worried about gangrene. I'll wash it at the spring every day. In a few days you won't even be able to see it."

I wasn't going to let a little thing like a small cut ruin my big day. I was finally a real hunter!

CHAPTER TWENTY

Bounty Of The Earth

The entire family realized that survival through the coming winter depended on replenishing essential household supplies. Because we had no cash it was essential that we obtain furs to trade for flour, cornmeal, salt, gunpowder, bullets, and other commodities.

My older brothers had decided that any trapping done on the high plateau must be completed before drifts became too deep. Later in winter, when snows were too deep in the highlands, we would trap streams that drained the valley floor. However, trapping had to wait till pelts were prime—when an animal's fur is at its thickest and glossiest.

In late October, Warner and John began planning their trapping expedition to the highlands east of Sand Run. The first hard freeze had occurred in mid-October and ice covered the quiet pools of Sand Run on many mornings. Although snow had fallen on several days, only isolated patches had accumulated. From the front porch we could see several small drifts along the upper rim of the valley.

Two days before Warner and John were to begin their expedition to the high plateau, John and Zedekiah came across a partially-eaten wild turkey alongside Glade Run. The tracks were less than a day old and they were positive a wolf was the culprit.

At supper that night they explained how they would construct three or four wolf traps, similar to those used by Meshach Browning to capture bears. They would cut enough logs to complete one trap, and bait it with the turkey carcass and some bear grease.

The finished trap would be about four feet wide; four feet tall, and five feet long. A heavy door, consisting of three small logs, would drop when the wolf pushed against a heavy strip of leather after it entered the trap. They explained how the wolf would be alive and they would have to shoot it in the trap.

Both of my brothers dreamt of the bounty money they would collect, and what they would buy with it. John described the Sharps rifle he would buy, and Zedekiah proposed to buy more steel traps and a goodly supply of powder and ammunition with his share.

John said, "Zedekiah and I will build one trap tomorrow and the next day all four of us boys will go to Cabin Mountain and set the traps and gather enough firewood to last you a week. Zedekiah and I will return to check on the first wolf trap and build at least three more. Little Georgie can stay with you and keep the fire burning and grill meat for your meals. If you have any problems he can go for help."

I was so excited I could hardly contain myself. I said nothing, but waited anxiously for Dad's response.

Lizzie was the first to speak, "I know Little Georgie can gather firewood, keep a campfire burning, and even grill a rabbit over the fire, but do you think he's big enough to go for help if there's trouble?"

Warner answered, "Georgie knows how to handle an axe and a one-man crosscut saw and he could easily find his way off the mountain if necessary. I know how much bounty money we would collect from a dead wolf, and now seems an ideal time to initiate our wolf trapping efforts. I would feel comfortable with Georgie as my trapping partner."

Finally, John said, "What do you think, Georgie? Do you think you can handle all the necessary chores?"

Emphatically I answered, "I know I can do it and I promise I'll be extra careful with the axe and saw."

Finally Dad answered, "I have doubts about the youngster being alone all day on the mountain while you're checking your traps. He isn't even ten years old yet. But I guess you won't be too far away if he gets into trouble."

Thus, the matter was settled. I felt so proud that I couldn't speak.

On a cold, snowy morning in early November, Warner and I began our trapping adventure. Warner was convinced we could snare enough rabbits to provide all the food needed during our anticipated seven-day expedition. He explained that, if necessary, we would eat the meat of trapped bobcats, fisher, or foxes. Lizzie wrinkled her nose in disgust at this, since carnivore flesh was not as tasty as herbivores.

Because of the snow, there would be no grasses for the horses. Thus, the plan was for John and Zedekiah to assist with setting up camp and setting traps and snares. They would spend the night and then ride the horses back to the cabin the following morning. They would return with the horses in seven days to retrieve the camping equipment and, most importantly, the hundreds of pelts that Warner expected to collect.

Warner had selected a route that angled upward, rather than directly confronting the steep mountainside, and by late morning we were approaching the rim. Enormous black cherry and maples had dominated the lower sections of the mountain, but near the top we encountered stunted trees and shrubs, few exceeding ten feet in height. Warner explained that the prevailing westerly winds stunted tree growth at that elevation.

I was spellbound at the sight spreading before us when we finally reached the broad, relatively flat plateau. A few small stands of evergreens were scattered before us, but piles of boulders dominated. Some boulders were larger than our cabin. The snow had been only a few inches deep along Sand Run, but we encountered drifts nearly two-feet deep on the plateau.

Fortunately, large expanses of the plateau were wind-swept, and unless a snowstorm arrived in the next few days Warner and I should be able to trap unimpeded. Warner and John urged our horses towards a stand of red spruce where the small Confederate cabin was located.

Deep within the spruce stand, John and Warner cut spruce poles, and Zedekiah and I trimmed off their branches. In two hours we had added two large lean-tos to the small cabin, one for storing supplies and a second for storing furs.

Slanted backs of the lean-tos faced west and south, while the high, open sides faced the cabin walls. Tarpaulins and spruce branches covered the tops and ends of the shelters. A fire within the cabin would provide warmth, and another small fire at the end of the fur-storage lean-to would accommodate smoking of meat.

John began to have mixed emotions about the wolf trapping and even mentioned that he might stay with Warner and send me home with Zedekiah. However, when Warner reminded him about the wolf bounty John dropped any ideas of remaining on the mountain.

John and Warner were eager to set traps, but realized it was more important to gather firewood. While hauling wood we also collected red maple branches for the horses. Although not highly nutritious the woody browse would fill their stomachs.

At dusk, we retreated to the shelter of the cabin. Following supper of dried beef and day-old bread we crawled, fully dressed, beneath blankets and bearskins. The soft layer of balsam fir and red spruce branches beneath us provided comfort and a pleasant scent.

Temperatures dropped below freezing during the night, and while Warner and John rekindled the fires at daylight, I snuggled deeper beneath the blankets. However, as the tempting scent of bear bacon and stick bread reached me, I emerged from my cocoon.

Zedekiah and I were allowed to accompany our older brothers as they set traps and snares that first frigid morning on the plateau. During that outing, we were thrilled to discover the tracks of numerous furbearers. Most abundant were those of fisher, although we also identified fox, bobcat, and weasel. The distinct tracks of rabbits were also present. Most intriguing, however, were some rabbit-like tracks that were nearly twice the size of rabbit tracks along the Potomac River.

Warner commented, "Either giant rabbits live on these mountains, or the tracks were made by those rabbit-like animals Cosner called hares."

We set forty steel traps that first morning before John and Zedekiah left, and Warner and I set thirty wire snares by the end of the day. Warner decided I would be responsible for checking the snares, while he concentrated on the steel traps. Thus, all snares were set near camp so I would not have far to travel. This would enable me to return to the camp, keep the fires burning, and cook.

By mid-day, John and Zedekiah had left with the horses. The family had expressed great interest in the camp where Warner and

I would spend the next six days. I reminded John to tell them about all the trails, tracks, and dropping left by the hares. Warner suggested they assure the family that we should have no problem snaring all the hares we could eat.

I added, "Tell Caroline we will bring back several hares for her to make a big stew."

CHAPTER TWENTY-ONE

Big Brother

Warner and I had settled into a regular routine by the end of the second day. We awoke, rekindled the fire, set a kettle of water on to boil, propped leftover meat from the previous evening over flames then readied our packs in preparation for checking traps and snares. When the water in our black kettle boiled, we made mugs of tea, leaned back against the short logs we had dragged into the cabin, and enjoyed breakfast.

Then we set off on our daily rounds—Warner to check steel traps and I to visit the snares. The traps were set in a circle around the cabin, between one-fourth and one-half mile distant, reducing the chance our camp sounds and smells would frighten furbearers. Because rabbits and hares were less suspicious, we felt confident in setting snares within a few hundred yards of camp.

Quite a surprise greeted me when I checked my snares that first morning on the mountain. The first six were empty, but the seventh held a hare. I could not believe my eyes. It was white! Not brown like the cottontail rabbits that frequented the blackberry thickets throughout the Potomac Valley, but white as the snow drifts that characterized its winter home on the Allegheny Plateau. In addition, its hind feet were noticeably larger than were the cottontail's, earning it the common name of snowshoe hare.

I typically returned around mid-day, whereas Warner would not complete his round until mid-afternoon. After lunch we began the finger-freezing task of skinning the animals which had been skidded back to camp on ropes and leather thongs. Furbearers, such as foxes, fisher, bobcats, and weasels, were easy to skin, with little danger of tearing the hides.

Hare hides were the most fragile of all the mammals we captured and extreme care was necessary in their handling. The sleek pelts were hung on wooden pegs. Later we would scrape each one to remove fat and flesh.

Meaty carcasses were gutted, and then head, feet, and tailbone removed. Hares were suspended several feet above the fire and preserved in the smoke, or positioned on a spit just above the flames to cook slowly. The last task of the afternoon was to cut logs into short sections, three to four feet long, for burning inside the cabin. Twenty to thirty such sections were dragged into the cabin each night and stacked against a wall where they would be within easy reach during the night.

With a deep pile of coals in the fire pit and comforting flames throwing orange light throughout the cabin, we relaxed for the first time that day. We discussed our strategy for the next day. Warner described how he planned to reposition some of his traps, and suggested I search the area surrounding the cabin for other hare trails. We seldom stayed awake long after supper, deeply exhausted from the day's activities. I usually slept ten to twelve hours each night.

By the fourth day, the excitement of finding a snowshoe hare in one of my snares lessened somewhat. I still approached each snare with great anticipation, and was always disappointed when it was empty.

In contrast, the presence of a dead hare never failed to excite me. I felt a sense of accomplishment in knowing I had successfully set the snare in just the precise location and manner necessary to outsmart a hare. My returning to camp with four or five hares trailing along at the end of a rope was something I often wished my family could see.

It snowed three consecutive days, but not enough to seriously limit our daily travels. Temperatures remained below freezing, both day and night, but not low enough to pose a threat of frostbite. With plenty of firewood available, we stayed warm. By the end of the week, Warner estimated we had burned enough logs to completely fill the cabin.

Our appetites were enormous, and together we typically ate three to four hares each day. On the fourth day, as we tired somewhat of hare, Warner suggested we try another meat. He explained, "We're on a grand adventure, and we must make this the most memorable of your life."

In considering what meat to cook, Warner said, "We have bobcat, fox, and fisher carcasses hanging on the cabin wall. Which do you want to try first?"

Rarely had my family eaten the flesh of carnivores. We had eaten lots of raccoons, but everyone knows they are not strictly meat eaters, consuming corn, grapes, persimmons, acorns, and chestnuts. I frowned and answered, "I really don't want to try any of them. But I might eat a little so I can brag to John and Zedekiah. Why don't we try the bobcat? The flesh is lighter in color than that of fox and fisher, and seems to resemble raccoon."

Thus, on the afternoon of the fifth day we tied a bobcat carcass to a maple pole and stretched it on a spit over the fire. With each end of the pole neatly suspended in the forks of a maple sapling, it was easy to turn the carcass and cook all sides evenly.

After two hours, the legs bent easily, indicating the meat was cooked to the bone. My brother ran a whetstone over the blade of his hunting knife several times and neatly sliced a long strip of backstrap (also called tenderloin) from along the backbone. After handing it to me, he removed the other backstrap for himself.

I sniffed curiously at my piece, and waited for Warner to take the first bite. Watching intently, I studied the expression on his face as he began chewing. I thought his nose curled up slightly, but I couldn't be certain. As he swallowed the first bite, he urged, "Now it's your turn. That bite was not half bad."

I answered, "If it's not half bad, that means it could be all bad."

Warner smiled and responded, "You'll just have to find out yourself."

I bit a chunk from the backstrap and chewed tentatively. Much to my surprise, it was almost good. The only problem was the odor. It may have been my imagination, but I was certain I could detect cat odor. Regardless, we consumed both backstraps and the two front legs that evening. The hind legs were separated from the hip girdle, to be eaten the next morning.

As we wiped the grease from our hands and settled back to enjoy our birch tea, I suggested, "If we trap another bobcat, why don't we save its backstraps and legs and ask Caroline to roast them in the oven. We won't tell anyone what they are and will let them guess when the meat is served."

Warner thought that was a wonderful idea.

We saw limited wildlife while trapping, although chickadees, blue jays, and woodpeckers were common in the spruce stands around our camp. A golden eagle flew over several times each day, and I saw a weasel sniffing around the carcasses we had hanging on the cabin wall.

My mid-morning snack on the second day was interrupted by a melodious croak heard above the whistling wind. Flying along the ridgeline was a most amazing bird. It was a raven.

The bird was riding air currents, at times remaining almost motionless as it flew into a gust. Two ravens flew past, but quickly turned as they spotted me. They swooped toward me and circled several times, while emitting their resounding croaks. Eight other ravens soon joined them.

After satisfying their curiosity, they began a fascinating aerial show. They performed in pairs, with one folding its wings and diving steeply while the second followed closely behind. The first raven would roll on its back and give several rusty-door croaks, and the two birds seemed to make physical contact before pulling out of the dive. The show continued for almost thirty minutes, with as many as six birds simultaneously diving at once.

Ravens were constant visitors since they were attracted to the gut piles we dumped a short distance from the cabin. One seemed to follow me on my rounds of checking snares, prompting me to imagine raising a pet raven if we could find a nest the following spring. I reckoned it wouldn't be too different from raising a crow.

In reliving the Cabin Mountain trapping expedition, as I liked to call it, one rewarding aspect stood out above others. It was not the animals we trapped, or the unbelievable scenery, or the challenges we overcame, or even the bobcat we ate. It was the companionship. Sometime around the fifth day, I realized I had never been alone with an adult for such a long period of time.

From the time Warner returned to camp each afternoon until I went to sleep, we worked together, ate together, and talked together. I was amazed how easy it was to talk to Warner. We talked about our family, our life in the Potomac Valley, our Canaan home, and our future.

I said, "I'll forever be grateful to Dad for bringing us to this Canaan Wilderness. We have so many exciting adventures to look forward to. What a wonderful life we have ahead of us."

Warner agreed, but cautioned, "I'm a little concerned about being able to clear enough land to grow crops and produce all the vegetables we'll need to survive the winter. It appears we'll run short of potatoes, cabbage, and squash for the next couple winters. No one likes to eat only meat, but that's what we may face."

I grew comfortable expressing my thoughts to Warner and on the sixth night revealed something that had been on my mind every day of our trapping expedition. "Please don't tell John and Zedekiah, or anyone else in our family, but I don't want to kill the female wolf. I realize the cash bounty would buy a new rifle, lots of gunpowder and ammunition, plus several sacks of cornmeal and flour, but I dream of having a wolf pup."

Warner said nothing, and I continued. "I've spent hours trying to decide what I would name the wolf pup. I don't want a sissy name like Lucy or Bonnie. People's names will work for dogs, but a wolf needs a wild-sounding name. I want a powerful name, one that will reflect its size and strength and faithfulness."

After reflecting on my seriousness, Warner finally spoke. He didn't make fun of me, like my other brothers would have if the entire family had been present. Instead, Warner made serious suggestions. "You should come up with an original name, one that has never been given to a wolf or a dog—one that reflects strength or stamina or faithfulness or disposition. What about Mountain or Rocky or Thunder or Timber or Killer? Or possibly Stormy or Hickory?"

I was surprised at Warner's seriousness, and for the first time in my life realized I could discuss matters with an adult. Some in my family might have considered me a youngster, not old enough to do my share of work, but Warner seemed to accept my ideas as he would those of an adult. I felt so content, and so pleased, to be camping with Warner.

CHAPTER TWENTY-TWO

Deadly Steel Traps

Zedekiah and John rode their horses into the camp atop Cabin Mountain—as Lizzie had named it—on a day with a clear blue sky and dazzling snow cover. Warner had checked and retrieved the traps while I did the same for the snares. The two of us were skinning the night's bounty as our brothers jumped off the horses.

Warner explained that we had captured one weasel and a fox the first night, but our disappointment in not capturing more furbearers was tempered by finding six large rabbits and one small fisher in the snares.

Warner announced that he had trapped three bobcats, ten foxes, and fifteen fishers during the week. I proudly stated that I had snared thirty-two snowshoe hares. Fifteen hares had been butchered and their disjointed quarters frozen and packed into burlap sacks. These were to be a surprise for the rest of the family, who had not enjoyed fried rabbit since we left the Potomac Valley.

Sounding as mature as possible, I repeated what Warner and I had discussed, "The soft white furs will be tanned and converted into warm blankets or coats for Daniel and little Emma."

I nervously asked the question that had been on my mind since John and Zedekiah left us a week ago, "Did you trap the wolf?"

John frowned, and answered, "We built four log traps, but never could entice the wolf to enter. That wolf must have learned to avoid human structures. We'll wait until late winter, when it's really hungry, and set the traps again." Although disappointed for my brothers, I thrilled to know the wolf was still alive.

Sacks containing our remaining food, supplies, and cooking utensils were strapped across the horses' backs alongside pelts rolled into compact bundles. With Mac and Abe plodding slowly down the mountainside, my three brothers and I walked cheerfully alongside. Dad was cutting firewood on the hillside overlooking Sand Run. Hearing our noisy caravan he hurried to the cabin and announced our return.

Everyone was eager to see the pelts. The luxurious bobcat furs brought countless words of praise, but the snowy white hare pelts garnered the most attention. It was impossible for everyone to resist running their hands through the amazingly soft furs.

Lizzie demanded, "I must have a coat made of these white furs! With such a garment I could tolerate howling winds and freezing temperatures."

Caroline quietly offered, "They certainly would make warm coats or extra warm blankets for the youngsters."

Dad calmly asked, "Would you rather have flour and cornmeal or coats and blankets? You may have to make the choice when we get ready to take the furs to market."

We spent the next week scraping every last bit of flesh from the pelts and stretched them to dry. They would be stored in the rafters of the barn, out of reach of hounds, until taken to market. The delicate pelts of the snowshoe hares were carefully scraped and then exposed to dense hemlock smoke; thus starting the tanning process.

Snows fell regularly throughout the first two weeks of November, but accumulations did not exceed two feet. While difficult to walk through, the drifts didn't prevent the completion of our everyday chores. Eggs were gathered, cows were milked, livestock were fed, and, most demanding of all, firewood was hauled, cut, and split.

We began trapping in the valley the third week of November. Warner and John again loaded the horses and headed for Glade Run, where they planned to remain for at least five days. Grasses grew plentiful on both sides of the meandering stream and the hobbled horses could eat red maple twigs or dig through the snow and reach all the dried forage they needed.

Zedekiah and I were allotted Sand Run and the Blackwater River. We worked as a team, setting traps along Sand Run one day and along the Blackwater River the next. Because there were no rabbits or hares living on the valley floor we didn't bother to set snares.

Thereafter, we planned to work alone to check the traps. Dad thought we should go together to check traps, but both Zedekiah and I wanted to work alone. I wanted to prove to the family that I was old enough to run a trap line by myself. Dad insisted we each carry a rifle when checking traps. Although the extra weight and bulk would slow us down considerably, we agreed. I would take my muzzleloader and Zedekiah would take the Sharps. Dad also warned me about being careful with my hunting knife. "Remember what happened when you were skinning the deer early in the fall? You could have bled to death before anyone found you. Sometimes I think you're followed by a cloud of bad luck."

Confidently I answered, "I'll only be cutting off their hides and won't have to reach my hands inside like I did gutting that deer. Besides, I'll be extra careful."

I could hardly wait! I would be responsible for checking the traps every day, removing any captured animals, and resetting traps. I figured there was little to worry about unless I got caught by an unexpected snowstorm or fell into one of Sand Run's deep holes. I later realized that overconfidence is a terrible trait.

Every morning for the next five days, I headed south to check traps along the upper reaches of Sand Run, while Zedekiah headed west to the Blackwater. We returned by early afternoon. The small animals we trapped, the weasels and mink, were carried home in a burlap sack thrown over our shoulder. Larger animals, such as fox and fisher, were skinned where trapped, then dragged home on a rope, sliding easily atop the snow.

Sad to say, we didn't have a lot of luck. Zedekiah trapped two mink, one fisher, and a raccoon. Through the first three days I managed to trap only one mink and one raccoon. On the fourth day, one of my traps held a bobcat. Their pelts were worth more than the others and I was overjoyed. I figured that if I caught a couple more of the handsome cats, my pelts might be worth enough to trade for a cartridge-shooting rifle.

After carefully skinning the bobcat, with no unnecessary cuts in the pelt, I added fresh bait and began the dangerous task of resetting the steel trap. Placing the trap on a fallen log, I held one jaw down with my foot and pushed the other jaw down with my right hand. My left hand needed to be free to secure the pan—the final action that held the jaws open.

If I had been stronger I could have safely held the jaws apart. Warner and John accomplished the feat with almost no effort. Ice had accumulated on the thick jaws and as I struggled to maintain control of the powerful trap, my foot slipped, and the jaws slammed shut on my right hand. Fortunately, I wore heavy leather mittens over wool liners, but my fingers were clamped tight, behind the second and third joints.

My fingers didn't seem to be broken, but I couldn't be certain. Regardless, the pain was excruciating. There was no way I could open the jaws of the trap with my left hand. After much thought, however, I concluded Zedekiah and Dad would certainly come searching for me, and could easily follow my tracks in the snow. I calculated they would find me in less than two hours, just as darkness arrived.

Although convinced this was not a life-threatening situation, I realized frostbite was possible. I remembered the story Dad told of his uncle Gerald who suffered serious frostbite in his feet when he fell through ice covering the South Branch River. Gangrene developed in his legs and he died within three weeks.

Nearly all of the Leatherman family had accidents, but it seemed like I took the brunt of them. John had smashed his thumb with a hammer. A log had rolled onto Warner's foot, but it was only a sprain. Belle, our Jersey cow, kicked Zedekiah while she was being milked, leaving an ugly bruise on his ankle. Lizzie was stung dozens of times when searching for a honeybee hive. Daniel burned his hand on a hot skillet.

My only way out was to detach the trap from the sapling and make my way home with the trap still clamped onto my right hand.

Unfortunately, the chain attached to the end of the steel trap was anchored securely to a hemlock sapling by a piece of wire.

Focusing my attention on the anchor wire, I attempted to untwist it, but to no avail. My mittens and woolen liners were too bulky. I removed the gloves from my left hand and attempted to untwist the wire that anchored the trap. After several futile attempts, I realized another approach was needed.

I certainly did not want to remove the wool liner from my left hand. Desperately removing my skinning knife from its leather, I attempted to pry apart the ends of the wire. But I was working left-handed and struggled to control the knife tip. If I could not release the trap chain with my left hand, I would be forced to wait until Dad and Zedekiah came to my rescue. That would be embarrassing and I would lose any respect I might have garnered if I couldn't release myself from the trap and return on my own.

Renewing my efforts with the knife, I slowly pried apart the ends of the wires, but could not grasp them with my fingers. In desperation, I removed my woolen liner and slowly untwisted the wires. The fingers of my left hand were so numb I could not feel the cuts created by the ends of the jagged wires, and I ignored the blood that trickled onto the sparkling white snow.

After what seemed to be at least an hour, the anchor chain finally dropped free. I forced my left hand inside my woolen coat and under my right armpit. Slowly the feeling returned and I stopped worrying about frostbite in that hand. However, the numbness in the fingers of my right hand had spread upward into my wrist.

With the bobcat hide thrown over my shoulders, the muzzleloader in my left hand, and the steel trap dangling from my right hand, I began the struggle back down Sand Run to our cabin. I could have waited until help arrived, but the nearer I was to our cabin; the sooner I would be found.

With boyish confidence, I began the journey homeward. Although the snow was only one foot deep, a slight crust had formed the previous night. The crust had been strong enough to support my weight when I began checking traps, although I did break through every so often.

But with the extra weight of the bobcat hide and the steel trap I broke through on nearly every step. With each step my weight was temporarily held atop the crust, but as I shifted my balance onto the other foot, I sank into the snow.

One-foot-deep snow would normally not be a major deterrent, but three rest stops were necessary before I had covered 100 yards. I had nearly a half-mile to reach the cabin. The struggle would be more difficult than I had thought.

If I were to successfully reach our cabin, I must lighten my load. I had only two choices; leave the bobcat hide or the rifle. They weighed nearly the same, about ten pounds. I could have reduced the weight of the hide if I had cut off all four legs and the head, but that would have reduced its value. Besides, I might need the hide to keep me warm.

While resting under a large hemlock, I decided to abandon the muzzleloader. I leaned it against the tree trunk, figuring I could come back to get it in the morning.

With my weight reduced, I no longer broke through the snow crust at each step. Now I was able to complete ten to fifteen steps before awkwardly plunging downward. I cradled the trap in my left arm, thus reducing the pain in my right hand and arm. After an hour of slow travel, I was only half way home.

The sun had set when I plopped unceremoniously against a hemlock. I reasoned that a ten-minute rest would rejuvenate my strength. However, I quickly dozed off and thirty minutes later was still slumped there. Although the numbness had inched from my right fingers into my hand and then into my arm, I slept soundly.

The next day, Zedekiah revealed all the details of the anxiety inside our cabin and the worried search that followed when I did not return home at the normal time. Zedekiah had nervously paced through the small cabin, and ventured down to Sand Run on several occasions after returning from checking his trap line along the Blackwater. Finally, with daylight fading fast, Dad announced, "I guess we better go see what happened to that boy. It's going to be a cold night and I doubt he wants to spend it outside."

Lizzie was more concerned than anyone. She firmly proclaimed,

"I'm going with you. If he's hurt I can help. He would want me to come. I know."

But Dad firmly ordered, "No. Zedekiah and I can find him. You would only slow us down. You can help by having some warm broth and corn pone ready when we return."

Caroline muttered, "That young'un still has a cloud floating over his head."

Fortunately, I had described in detail the area where I was trapping. Zedekiah was familiar with the area and led the rescue. They were able to follow my tracks made that morning. Both knew they would find me, but were still concerned. They knew I was in trouble, because I had returned around midday on other trapping days.

Zedekiah told me they broke through the snow crust at each step, and were forced to take turns breaking trail. After traveling steadily for nearly an hour, they stopped to rest. Dad announced, "If we don't find him by dark, we must return home. It's not safe wandering around here with no light. We certainly don't want to fall and break a leg. I sure wish there was a moon."

Zedekiah did not agree, but said nothing. He thought I could not survive the night, and I must be found before temperatures dropped further. His conviction was strengthened when the howl of a timber wolf floated eerily across the valley. The howl was repeated a second time and, a few minutes later, a third time. But no answering response was triggered.

Zedekiah said he told Dad, "If that wolf is near it could pick up Georgie's scent. We can't take a chance of that happening. We must find Georgie, and the sooner the better."

After a five-minute rest, Zedekiah and Dad rose and followed the faint outline of my tracks. They traveled less than 100 yards when they lost the trail. With a lantern they might have been able to detect my tracks, but darkness and the new snow were too much to overcome. Zedekiah started yelling, "Georg...ie, Georg...ie, Georg...ie." Had I been awake I could have easily heard it. But I was asleep, dreaming of a warm cabin and an even warmer supper.

Dad announced, "We'll go another ten minutes and call again."

After the planned interval, they both yelled together, coordinating their efforts.

Fortunately, I was roused from sleep by the pain extending up my right arm. Not certain if I was dreaming, I removed my woolen hat and turned my head to face the direction of the sound. Was the call real or imagined? Hearing nothing, I replaced my hat and once again fell into a light sleep.

Zedekiah said he pleaded to Dad, "Five more minutes. Let's go five more minutes."

Dad said nothing, but resumed their search. Certain they were getting closer with each step, Zedekiah vowed to call even louder. After a few minutes, they again coordinated their call, "Georg…ie. Georg…ie. Georg…ie."

I suddenly jerked alert, certain I had indeed heard voices. My voice sent forth a weak answer, "Here…, Here…, Here." Then after an anxious wait, I repeated my response, "Here…, Here."

Zedekiah told Dad, "I heard him. I know I did. Let's hurry."

They quickly pushed through the snow towards my calls. Another call from Zedekiah and a response from me resulted in their spotting me under the hemlock. As they approached, I calmly announced, "I trapped a nice bobcat, but I had a little trouble with the trap."

Zedekiah responded, "I sure am glad to see you. I thought you might be injured badly, or dead."

Dad added, "Are you hurt? Why are you sitting here?"

The bobcat skin concealed the trap. As I rose from the ground, the skin fell to the ground. Zedekiah asked, "Why are you holding that big old heavy trap?"

I answered, "I'm not holding it. It's holding me."

Working together, Dad and Zedekiah quickly released my fingers from the trap and lifted me to my feet. Zedekiah carried the bobcat skin and the trap while Dad slipped his arm around my waist and held me upright as we headed for home.

Fortunately, they had created a relatively open trail in the snow, and we made good time. By the time we caught sight of the firelight flickering through the cabin window I had regained some strength.

Dad helped me climb the hill from Sand Run to our cabin. The family came rushing to the door. Seeing me standing there, apparently healthy, Lizzie asked, "What happened to you? Why didn't you come home? I've been worried nearly sick about you."

Zedekiah tossed the beautiful bobcat pelt on the floor of the cabin and immediately little Emma picked it up and began stroking its soft fur.

I headed for the fireplace, anxious to examine my hand. It was still numb and I knew it must have suffered serious injury. Of most concern was my index finger, my shooting finger. Without a shooting finger, I could do no more hunting. It would take years to master shooting with my off hand.

Everyone crowded close as I removed the mitten and glove from my right hand. Lizzie nearly gagged when she saw the ugly, purple crease across the middle three fingers and the red streaks extending up the back of my hand onto my wrist.

Caroline commanded, "Get a pan of warm water. He must soak his hand immediately. We must stop gangrene from developing."

I didn't like being the center of such attention, and casually responded, "It doesn't hurt. I don't even think any bones are broken."

After soaking it while eating hot venison broth and butter-soaked corn bread, I went to bed. As the numbness wore off, pain appeared, and I concluded that bones could indeed be broken. I tossed and turned all night, worried about what I would learn the next day when I tried using my right hand.

The pain was worse the next morning, but the color of my fingers and hand had returned to normal. There were, however, a few nasty red streaks on the back of my hand. Caroline constantly urged me to soak the hand in warm salt water.

I was forced to stay in the house for five days, at the end of which time I had regained partial use of the fingers and hand. I had nothing to do and boredom set in. We were not certain whether I should be using my fingers, or soaking them, or letting them rest.

A week after my little adventure, Dad said I could help carry in firewood. He added, "Try small pieces at first, and if your hand doesn't hurt too bad you can try larger ones."

The last week of November was rainy—unfit weather to hunt. Dad said we should cut and split more firewood, stating, "Firewood is like money. You can never have too much. We don't want to be cutting firewood when the snow is six feet deep."

I wasn't strong enough to maneuver one end of a two-man crosscut saw or split wood with a double-bitted axe, but I could stack wood onto the horse-drawn sled. We concentrated on sugar maple and black cherry, two hardwoods that produced long-lasting hot coals. With five of us working, we typically loaded the sled by noon, returned to the cabin for a change of clothes and a big mid-day meal, and then returned to work until dark.

By the end of November my fingers had returned to normal, although there was considerable pain when I attempted carrying a bucket of water from the spring. At least I was not going to suffer from gangrene.

Unfortunately, my hand had not returned to full strength and my trapping season came to an end. I was disappointed that I had not harvested enough pelts to buy a cartridge rifle, but I would have enough to buy adequate powder and lead for the winter hunting season.

While loafing around the cabin, waiting for my fingers to heal, I relived the many adventures that had highlighted my short life. It occurred to me that most of my memories centered on tragic events: the death of my mother, a head injury resulting from a fall, my poison ivy experience, the knife cut to my hand, the failure of our crops, and my encounter with the steel trap. I wondered whether my life had been a series of disasters, with few joyous events, or did my memory more readily store, and revive, the negative events. I reasoned that a person immediately recognizes the potential consequences of disastrous events. In contrast, the benefits of joyous events are short-lived, or not apparent until months or even years later—and thus not stored as memories.

I concluded that the joyous times in my life had indeed been few and far between. They were often brief events, enjoyable but not life-changing. In contrast, calamitous events had immediate consequences, such as pain, healing, and long-term, permanent impacts in the form of scars and limited physical movements.

In the wilderness, tragic times certainly outweigh happy times. By the time my fingers were healed, I had concluded that such potentially disastrous events should be considered adventures, not tragedies. Not something to regret, but something to revel in having survived.

A wilderness such as Canaan Valley presented challenges, and trials, and excitement. The death of any human was indeed tragic, but surviving disasters and near-disasters offered a reward unlike anything life in a civilized area could ever provide.

CHAPTER TWENTY-THREE

Blood In The Snow

Lone Wolf, as we named her, and my family peacefully coexisted during the fall of 1880. We heard her lonesome howls on many nights during summer and spotted her tracks along beaver ponds in Glade Run.

I encountered Lone Wolf a second time while searching for promising places to hunt turkeys. While crossing a small tributary of Sand Run I spotted movement out of the corner of my eye. Cautiously dropping to one knee and slowly swinging my rifle barrel toward the movement, I anxiously searched the grasses. Suddenly, there it was! A wolf, staring directly at me! It was within shooting range and didn't run.

It seemed curious rather than fearful. I was in awe of its beautiful silvery fur, and its powerful head, and even its penetrating stare. Subconsciously I lowered my rifle; confident it was Lone Wolf. After a few minutes, the wolf disappeared from view. One second it was there and the next it was gone. A strange feeling swept over me. I imagined the wolf attempting to communicate. And I also imagined a wolf pup walking faithfully at my side.

Snows during October and November had provided excellent opportunities for deer and bear hunting. By the end of November, four deer, seven bears, and ten wild turkeys were hanging inside our smokehouse. Plans were to shoot one or two of the semi-wild cattle in lower Glade Run in mid-December and haul them back to our smokehouse with a horse-drawn sled. However, until the snows reached two feet deep we would continue hunting deer and turkey within a mile or two of our cabin.

Temperatures dropped sharply the third day of December and

snow replaced the rain. The afternoon of the fourth was spent preparing for the next day's hunt, sharpening knives and oiling rifles. Packs were loaded with ammunition, extra wool gloves and socks, and plenty of sourdough bread and smoked venison. Five of us would go, Dad, Warren, John, Zedekiah, and I. While sharing a hearty supper of wild turkey, corn bread, and buttermilk we determined hunting tracts. Snow stopped falling during the night, and temperatures remained just below freezing. While tossing and turning on my bed of balsam fir boughs, I constantly inventoried my supplies for the hunt.

About five a.m. Dad awoke, carefully placed three small logs atop the fireplace coals and started a small fire in the cooking stove. When flames from the fireplace threw a warm glow throughout the cabin, Caroline rose and began preparing our breakfast.

This was to be the day I died! I wish I had known, so I could have told Lizzie how much I loved her. I might have even told Caroline I was sorry for putting the puffing adder in her egg basket. That little prank still brought a smile every time I thought of it.

By the light of the fire and two flickering bear-tallow candles we ate a hearty breakfast of buckwheat cakes, fried venison steaks, hot biscuits, and a small serving of scrambled eggs.

After carrying in a day's supply of firewood for the cabin, we put on layers of wool pants, shirts, and jackets over our long-john underwear and hurriedly exited the cabin before we began to sweat.

Warner and I headed for Sand Run while the others went their agreed-upon directions. Stars were twinkling brightly in the crisp night sky as Warner and I crossed the bridge and moved silently up the slope above Sand Run.

In less than thirty minutes clouds rolled in and snow began to fall. Shortly after, we reached a small drain that flowed east into Glade Run, and Warner and I parted. Warner's last words—the last words I would ever hear—were, "Don't shoot anything too big or we can't drag it home."

I worked my way down off Middle Ridge along the scattered hemlocks until I reached the edge of the woods bordering the open glade. I began searching for a fallen tree where I could hunker until shooting light arrived. I selected a fallen giant black cherry tree and quietly packed the snow to form a resting spot. I carried a rolled up wool blanket around my shoulders and a tanned, hair-covered deer hide. Folding the deer hide to form a waterproof seat, I settled into a comfortable position against the fallen tree with the muzzleloader resting across my lap. The wool blanket covered my legs and most of the rifle. Only the butt of the wooden stock and the end of the iron barrel were exposed to the falling snow.

Now the wait began. If my feet didn't get too cold I always enjoyed this quiet time. My senses sharpened as I searched anxiously for the slightest sound or scent.

During warm weather I often dozed during this interval, to be wakened by the cracking of a limb, the snorting of a deer, the clucking of a wild turkey, or the scratching of bark as some wild critter climbed a nearby tree. But on this day, December 5, 1880, all was quiet. Sounds not muffled by the snow were buffeted by the swirling wind. I reckoned that most animals had fed during the night, aware that a storm was imminent. If so, most would bed down until late morning then resume feeding.

I remained confident of a successful hunt, due in part to my secret weapon—a urine-splattered deer hide. While field dressing a doe he shot in late November, Warner had carefully removed the bladder. The urine could be used to cure deer hides, but the smelly liquid could also be used to attract bucks—a hunting technique he had learned from Meshach Browning, one of the most successful hunters who ever wandered the Allegheny Mountains. Warner suggested I wrap the hide around my shoulders while stalking, thus breaking my outline and covering my scent.

In less than an hour my feet were so cold they hurt. Snow continued to fall and now covered the blanket shielding my lap, legs, and feet. The only means of driving out the cold and regaining even a small amount of warmth to my toes was walking. I left the shelter of the fallen tree and eased northward along the forest edge.

Quietly moving from tree to tree, while searching for movement, I attempted to simulate a hunting predator. I had frequently observed foxes moving along the edge of Sand Run, stopping and starting while ever alert for an unsuspecting bird, rabbit, or rodent. If the technique provided a meal for a fox then it should provide one for me.

By mid-morning I had covered several hundred yards but I had seen nothing except for a couple fairy-diddles, a downy woodpecker, and a small flock of chickadees.

My heartbeat increased when I saw the tracks of a bear, heading westward up onto Middle Ridge. I desperately wanted to follow the tracks, but knew Warner was hunting along the ridge and would be more successful in getting a shot at the bear than I would.

Thirty minutes later I spotted three deer grazing on cured grasses along Glade Run. The wind was coming out of the north, thus putting me downwind of the deer and making it easier to approach close enough for a shot.

When I had closed to within two hundred yards I realized the deer had turned their tails to the wind and were facing in my direction. This would make my stalk more difficult, but the blowing snow would help break my outline. Stopping behind a fallen sugar maple I patiently studied the behavior of the feeding deer. I thought I could see antlers on the largest of the three animals. I would have liked to shoot a large buck, but as Dad said, "No one eats antlers!"

With the wind to my face, I positioned the deer hide around my shoulders so it covered my back. The strips of hide that had covered the front legs were tied together so it could be worn like a cape, with the hind legs dragging the ground behind me. The hide that covered the deer's neck extended over my head.

Bending over to break my outline, I eased closer to my target. When I was a little over one hundred yards away, the deer moved toward Glade Run. I wanted to approach to within fifty yards and find a small sapling in which to rest my muzzleloader.

Unbeknownst to me, another hunter was moving along the banks of Glade Run, heading directly towards the same deer I was stalking. The hunter was two hundred yards upstream of me, and was just as determined as I.

The wind shifted direction and began blowing from the west, then increased velocity and swirled in small unpredictable eddies. Snowfall increased and visibility dropped to less than fifty yards. Earth blended with sky and sky blended with earth.

The other hunter moving along Glade Run that morning was Lone Wolf. My brothers had concluded that since the demise of her fellow pack members she had been forced to adapt the hunting style of a mountain lion. Had she belonged to a pack they would have pursued deer as a team, often in relays.

We often discussed, while sitting around the dinner table, Lone Wolf stalking small prey, deer fawns in summer, and snowshoe hare, wild turkeys, and weakened deer in winter. Other times, we figured, she waited patiently along a game trail, waiting to ambush some unsuspecting animal. Normally she would not have pursued adult deer, but hunger drives predators to abnormal behavior.

Following the encounter that snowy December day, I reconstructed the scene as it occurred along Glade Run. As she had often done on previous hunts, on this fateful day she would stalk close enough to the deer to determine if one might be injured and vulnerable to pursuit. If they appeared healthy she would abandon the pursuit and direct her efforts towards a juicy meadow vole.

Neither Lone Wolf nor I was aware of the other until the wolf detected the urine odor buffeting around Glade Run. Although unable to spot the source because of swirling snow, she began angling toward me. I sure wish I had known she was behind me. I might have tried to communicate with her, and try to let her know that I did not want to shoot her.

Lone Wolf most likely glided silently through the six-inch deep snow in my direction. When thirty yards away, she would have spotted my hunched form. Small clumps of snow clung to the deer hide and broke my outline. At twenty yards she began her charge. Each powerful leap covered eight feet. She launched her ninety-pound body into the air, targeting my right leg. She had learned not to aim for the neck because the slashing front hooves or antlers of an adult deer could cause serious injury.

While in mid-air, the wolf certainly detected human odor mixed with doe urine. Had she been given the luxury of even a few seconds to analyze the situation, she probably would have aborted the charge. But a hungry wolf must make instant decisions.

Lone Wolf made no sound other than exhaling gulps of oxygen-deprived air from her lungs. I was thrown to the ground at the same time I felt a sharp pain in my right knee. The inch-long fangs sliced through muscle and tendon and I immediately lost all use of my right leg.

The wolf instantly ceased her attack when my overpowering, unpleasant human odor permeated her nostrils. She was perplexed and dropped to her haunches and studied me quizzically. Our eyes met and held! Mine brown, wide open, and frightened. Hers were bluish-green, and intimidating. Her lips drew back from her teeth in a snarl, revealing four large, sharp canines.

I instinctively tried to swing the barrel of my muzzleloader in her direction, but with no success. It had fallen under me in the snow when I was knocked down. I attempted to pull my hunting knife from its sheath, but couldn't. I was doomed! Momentarily, I was awestruck by her strength and beauty. Her thick winter coat made her appear twice as large as the biggest hunting hound I had ever seen.

A deep, ominous growl escaped her powerful chest, and she crouched in preparation to charge. But no charge came. Lone Wolf hesitated. My human scent was so repulsive that she began to slink backwards, although continuing to snarl.

As her outline slowly dissolved into the swirling snow, I managed to retrieve the muzzleloader. Quickly pulling back the hammer, I pointed the barrel and pulled the trigger. My goal was to frighten her away and advise Warner of my location. Before I had time to reload the rifle, my body reacted to the shock of the attack and I passed out.

While unconscious, I dreamed of a massive wolf, slinking closer and closer through a snowstorm. Suddenly the wolf in my dreams leaped and clamped its jaws around my neck.

I eventually returned from the deep sleep, having been unconscious for nearly an hour. Possibly it was the pain in my right leg or my frostbitten toes and fingers that jolted me awake. Blood had soaked my woolen pants legs and stained a large patch of snow. I thought of Lizzie's paintings and weighed her appreciation of the contrast: white snow and red blood. The patch of crimson-stained snow was attractive enough to paint—or eat. I tried to stand, but fell awkwardly. The leg wouldn't support my weight.

I attempted to use the muzzleloader as a crutch, but fell again after only three shuffling steps. I clumsily reloaded the muzzleloader, omitting the lead ball, and fired it in the direction of the Middle Ridge. Pain could no longer keep me awake and I again slowly drifted into a deep sleep.

Warner had heard the first shot. A single shot typically meant success, while two shots were an indication the animal was not killed, but was fleeing the hunter. When he heard my second shot an hour later he was perplexed. After waiting for a third shot—a sure sign of trouble—he decided to see if I needed help.

He returned to the site where we had separated earlier that morning and carefully followed my tracks until spotting my body lying in the snow. He knew I was in bad trouble. My torn pant's leg revealed the injury and the wolf tracks in the snow revealed the culprit. Blood continued to flow from my wound, although at a slower rate than it had during the previous three hours.

Warner sliced long strips from the deer hide and bound my woolen pants tightly around the gaping wound, hoping to stop the bleeding. He constantly shook me during the entire time, urging me to regain consciousness. I was vaguely aware of Warner's words, but they faded into the distance as I fought to comprehend what was happening.

I was aware of Warner gently lifting me from the snow, balancing my body over his right shoulder, picking up both rifles in his left hand, and retracing his tracks back to the Middle Ridge trail. I weighed slightly over eighty pounds, but wore at least ten pounds of clothing. In addition, my muzzleloader weighed another ten pounds.

Warner struggled through the shin-deep snow with his 100-pound load. Fortunately, he was the huskiest of our family. Standing over six feet tall, he weighed 220 pounds. Regardless, I was an imposing burden.

After progressing less than one hundred yards, Warner slid my body off his shoulder into the snow and knelt for a rest. He was careful, but my head struck awkwardly and I regained consciousness. My eyes blinked open and closed, while Warner gently shook my shoulders from side to side. "Wake up Little Georgie! Wake up! Don't go to sleep or you'll never wake again! The bleeding has stopped. I'll get you home shortly! Stay with me!"

Barely conscious, I responded, "Don't kill the wolf. She thought I was a deer. I want one of her pups."

Warner held me in his arms and gently shook me, hoping I would stay awake. My eyes closed, opened briefly then closed again. Seconds later, my head drooped awkwardly onto my chest. I had lost too much blood. My human life came to an end, and on the morning of December 5, 1880, my spirit departed my earthly body.

Chapter Twenty-Four

Revenge

My spirit, as an uninvolved spectator, witnessed Warner carrying me back to the footbridge crossing Sand Run where he deposited our muzzleloaders, wool blankets, and leather knapsacks beneath a hemlock tree. After resting for nearly thirty minutes, he put my body over his shoulder and wearily made his way across the bridge and up the sloping hillside to the cabin. He climbed the cabin steps, crossed the porch, and kicked the door two times. "Open the door!" he weakly announced.

Caroline answered, "If you're carrying a dead deer, don't bring the bloody thing in here. Leave it on the porch."

Lizzie opened the heavy slab door, and gasped when she saw what Warner carried. She screamed, "It's Little Georgie! He's been hurt! Put him on the bed! Hurry!"

Warner carried me across the room, gently lay me onto the wool blankets, and awkwardly collapsed—saying nothing.

Lizzie had followed him to the bed and was removing my wool coat when she first detected my frozen, bloodless face. A gasp escaped her mouth, followed by a loud, ear-shattering scream, "He's dead! Georgie is dead!"

Daniel and little Emma came close to the bed, curious to see a dead person. Lizzie sobbed and shouted possessively, "Stay away! Don't touch him! He was my very best friend in the whole world! And now he's dead!" She stumbled around the room, from the bed to the fireplace, to the table, and back to the bed.

Caroline said nothing, while sitting silently at the table, shaking her head.

The cabin became quiet, as unbelieving minds wrestled with this shocking event, unwilling to accept death. There are some calamities too complex for those not present to ever visualize. For my family, this was one of those. I have oft wondered if there is any wilderness on earth where death is not the leading actor. One death can unite a family, but a second and a third will often lead to its destruction. Only time would tell how my family would survive this disaster.

Dad returned in mid-afternoon, followed shortly by Zedekiah. John entered the cabin as darkness cloaked Canaan—darkness unlike any my family had experienced. He had killed a large bear halfway up the mountain east of Sand Run. He had gutted it and planned to return the following day to fetch it. When each hunter returned to the cabin Warner repeated the details of my attack. He repeated my last words, "Don't kill the wolf. She thought I was a deer."

After eating a silent supper, Dad declared, "We must kill that wolf. I won't be satisfied until it is dead."

Lizzie responded, "But Georgie said he didn't want us to kill it."

My Dad answered, "Georgie was nearly unconscious when he mumbled those words. He didn't know what he was saying. We'll take the hounds tomorrow morning and follow them until we kill that murderer."

Nothing more was said. Before going to bed, Dad and Warner carried my body to the barn, and lifted me carefully into the hayloft. Nervously smoothing my temporary resting place of soft, fragrant hay, they spread a wool blanket over me.

Dad and my brothers rose before daylight on December 6, and after a silent breakfast Warner gathered our hounds. He and Dad would lead them to the site of my Glade Run attack; while John and Zedekiah would take a horse and skid the dead bear back to the cabin.

Snow had stopped the previous afternoon and Warner had no difficulty leading the hounds to the bright patch of blood-soaked snow. They quickly detected the wolf scent and with considerable excitement and dedication set off in silent pursuit. Ulysses had the best nose for tracking and, as usual, led the chase. Fury and Ranger followed closely behind. Warner and Dad were able to reconstruct many of the events following my attack by a careful examination of tracks in the snow.

Had it been summertime or even early autumn, Lone Wolf would probably have climbed the mountainside to her boulder den atop Cabin Mountain. However, with the arrival of low temperatures she kept her hunting along the valley floor, and used her Glade Run den. Prey, especially meadow voles, were more plentiful in the dense grasses bordering Glade Run than on the wind-swept plateau.

At the sound of my first muzzleloader shot she had turned tail and sped north. By the time sounds of my second shot echoed across the valley she had covered more than half a mile. Because no pain had been associated with the rifle shots she returned to her hunting.

Slowing to a walk, she called upon her smell and hearing. After a short stalk, she caught the heavy musky odor of a meadow vole, and soon targeted its bed within a clump of rice cutgrass. Springing nearly three feet into the air, she dropped onto the nest with well-directed front feet. Although cushioned by the soft snow, her front paws crushed the grassy nest and stunned the vole. Lone Wolf consumed the fresh meat in one gulp.

The wolf detected, but missed five meadow voles before being successful again. Two hours of intense hunting were required for Lone Wolf to capture five voles. Although not a filling meal, they helped her hunger pangs. The ever-shifting valley winds then brought her the odors of exposed flesh, dried blood, and spilled intestinal contents. The message was immediately translated into food. However, accompanying the deer-carcass odor was the odor of a mountain lion. After nearly forty minutes she approached to within twenty yards of the carcass. Circling the clump of meadowsweet, Lone Wolf was relieved that only faint lingering odors of mountain lion remained. The cat was not in the immediate vicinity.

A young male cougar had covered the deer carcass with snow, grass, and small branches after a meal of the best parts. Then he had slowly made his way up the mountainside to the safety of a den within a small pile of boulders. He would return the next day, and the day after that, to clean the last bits of flesh from the deer bones. But only enough venison for a small meal remained after Lone Wolf's feast. If a fox or fisher found the now-exposed carcass there would be little left for the cougar.

Lone Wolf was enjoying a deep sleep in her primary den west of Glade Run when Dad, Warner, and our hounds reached the deer carcass. In spite of the bitter temperatures outside, the wolf was quite comfortable. Her dense winter fur, which did not collect ice when warm air condensed against it, was resistant to cold as low as forty degrees below zero. With her muzzle snuggling between hind legs and her exposed face covered by a dense, bushy tail, the wolf was soon dreaming of another meal.

Had the snow been only a few inches deep, Dad and Warner could have distinguished between cougar and wolf tracks. Two sets of tracks led away from the deer carcass. One crossed Glade Run and headed towards Cabin Mountain. The other headed north, paralleling Glade Run. Neither humans nor hounds could determine which tracks the wolf had left.

Ulysses struck off after the cougar across Glade Run and up the mountainside, with Ranger and Fury following. Halfway to the top, Warner and Dad found where the cat had rested atop a wind-swept boulder. The clawless tracks, so representative of members of the cat family, were easily identified in the two inches of snow that clung to the boulder. Dad and Warner realized they had been following the wrong tracks.

Blowing the "come-back" call through the cow horn, which he carried on all hunts, Warner enticed the hounds to return. They then glumly retraced their tracks back to the deer carcass where they set off after the wolf.

In less than an hour the hounds were baying frantically at the mouth of the wolf's den. Ranger thrust his head and forequarters into the hole, but was hesitant to enter any deeper. The hounds were not anxious to crawl into the burrow. If the first hound to enter was killed, its body would form a barrier that would stop the other hounds. Dad and Warner had not brought a shovel and, besides, Dad was so determined to kill the wolf that he did not want to delay his revenge one minute longer than necessary.

Warner proposed they build a fire in the mouth of the den. Either the wolf would die from smoke inhalation, or would attempt to escape.

In that case, the hounds would overtake and kill it. After pulling Ranger bodily from the burrow, a small fire of dead spruce twigs was started in the entrance. To this, larger dead limbs were added, until a roaring fire developed.

I was surprised that my spirit could envision events that would not have been visible to a living human. Lone Wolf crouched nervously in her den, positioned fifteen feet from the entrance. The burrow itself was nearly two feet wide, providing easy passage for the wolf, but she felt secure in the den that had kept her warm and safe for the past two years.

She might have been able to survive the fire and smoke had it been a recently-built den; smoke would not have infiltrated deep enough to cause serious harm. But unfortunately, instinct had led her to build a secondary escape burrow that opened forty feet from the main entrance. And most unfortunately for her, the opening was slightly uphill of the den.

This escape tunnel and its associated elevated entrance created a chimney effect, which effectively pulled smoke from the fire through the burrow into the den. If Lone Wolf had slipped out the secondary opening when the first whiff of smoke seeped into her den she might have escaped. With all the commotion and thick smoke, it is doubtful that men or hounds would have spotted her speeding rapidly away.

In less than fifteen minutes, smoke began to drift from the secondary entrance. Warner spotted it and immediately grasped Ulysses by the collar and pulled him to the opening. Dad and the other two hounds waited at the primary entrance.

Loud barking now came from both entrances. Lone Wolf felt trapped. The eye-burning smoke was thicker in the tunnels than in the den, establishing a false sense of security. Crouching nervously against the rear wall of her den, Lone Wolf thrust her nose into the damp earth to escape the deadly smoke. She knew from experience that smoke occurred only in association with humans, whether from a cabin, a campfire, or a fire designed to remove unwanted trees. She was trapped!

Author's Addendum:

December 5, 1880, witnessed the first recorded death of a human in Canaan Valley and the following day, December 6, the last death of a wolf. Never again would barred owls warn nervous prey animals that a wolf was on the prowl. Never again would eerie wolf howls echo across the valley. Never again would a hungry wolf pull down a winter-weakened deer.

An integral element of the Appalachian wilderness had made its way into history. The ecosystem that wolves helped create was forced to adjust to this loss or be replaced by an entirely different system. White-tailed deer could eventually replace a prey base of elk and bison, but nothing would ever replace the overpowering sphere of influence thrust over the landscape by wolf packs.

And, there would never be another nine-year-old boy with such fantastic dreams about owning his own wolf pup.

CHAPTER TWENTY-FIVE

The Long Winter

Dad and Warner remained at the wolf den along Middle Ridge until late afternoon, constantly adding green hemlock branches to the fire. Warner was positive the wolf had succumbed to the smoke, and finally convinced Dad they could do nothing more.

Reluctantly, Dad agreed they would never know positively if they had killed the wolf. He finally concluded, "I guess if we don't hear any howls or spot any wolf tracks during the coming winter we'll know that either the wolf is dead or it left the area."

John and Zedekiah had returned with the dead bear and the skinned carcass was hanging in the smokehouse when Dad and Warner returned with the hounds. The spread bear hide was pegged onto the barn floor, where it would be scraped.

After Dad and Warner detailed their disappointing adventure, my family quietly consumed a supper of fresh bear liver and hot biscuits. Lizzie commented, "Georgie would be pleased that the wolf could possibly be alive."

My newly-released spirit had followed Warner as he nestled my lifeless body through the snow, across the footbridge, and into the cabin. Much to my surprise, I was aware of everything that happened and could even understand conversations. It was almost as if I were still alive.

December 6 became December 7. Following another gloomy meal that morning, Dad announced they would dig my grave that day, and line the sides and bottom with small-notched poles, creating a miniature log cabin.

The specific location of my grave caused considerable debate.

Lizzie was the most outspoken, stating, "It must be where I can see it from the cabin porch. Why don't we put it down near Sand Run? Georgie loved that stream since the brook trout are so plentiful. It can't be too far away since I want to visit it every day, rain or shine, sleet or snow."

No one else expressed an opinion. After an extended, awkwardly quiet period, Caroline spoke, "Graves should always be high on a hill. The spirits of the dead can look out over the land, while the surviving family can gaze upward at the grave, when working the fields or resting on the porch, gaining comfort in their personal recollections. Georgie must be put to rest with his feet towards the east, so he can see the rising sun easing over Cabin Mountain every morning for an eternity."

Her statement shocked the rest of the family. She had said nothing following my death, apparently feeling almost like an outsider because I was not her direct kin. Unfortunately, I had never considered her my mother, but I had come to accept her as an important person in our family. Although we depended on her meals, we rarely expressed our gratitude.

Lizzie responded, "The only site that fits that description is on the east-facing hillside overlooking Sand Run. It isn't higher than our cabin, but basically meets Caroline's description. The spot is about two hundred yards from our cabin and can be seen from our porch if I plant flowers on top."

Standing on the porch to gain the proper prospective, Lizzie directed Zedekiah to the spot she had in mind. Dad and my older brothers took turns digging, first shoveling off the snow then excavating deep into the sandy soil of Middle Ridge. They finished by lunchtime, returning shortly afterward to construct the internal framework of logs and large slabs of flattened bark.

I watched with interest, but felt no emotion. I realized that all lives come to an end, some after a few days, others after many years. But the result is the same. One more soul is released. There will be other lives, just as there will be other years. But possibly none with as much potential, just as no one life will be so memorable to the immediate family.

I realize now December was the best month to die for most early settlers. The year was over; they've seen all the animals born. The firewood was cut and stacked. The barn was full of hay and the smokehouse full of meat. They had a deep satisfaction that the year was productive. Death in December meant you didn't have to face the cold and hunger, the short, dark days of winter, the crowded life in the cabin, the trudging through deep snow to feed livestock, and the trips to the outhouse.

In mid-afternoon Lizzie and Caroline removed my gloves, hat, wool coat, shirt, wool pants, leather boots, and socks—everything except the blood-stained, one-piece underwear. Lizzie sobbed as she struggled to pry stiff clothes off even stiffer limbs. Life in the wilderness required that nothing be wasted. My clothing would be worn by Daniel, who was accustomed to wearing my hand-me-downs.

As Lizzie and Caroline finished their task, Lizzie proclaimed, "Georgie always loved wandering barefoot through the woods. He said it helped him understand the movements of deer and bears, and predict where they would travel."

Burial day was a spectacular, clear day, with sparkling ice crystals floating through the air, tree limbs cracking from the cold, and a pair of ravens croaking their respect. Warner and John carried my frozen body to the gravesite. Warner held my shoulders and head in his arms while John held my legs and feet, much as they hauled short logs into the cabin. I weighed significantly less than most logs tossed carefully into the fire, and either one of them could have carried me easily if he had thrown me over his shoulder.

Lizzie led the way to the site. A bed of spruce branches was laid at the bottom of the grave, and my barefoot body lovingly placed atop. A layer of soft balsam fir branches formed a covering blanket, which in turn was overlain with a large slab of bark from a tulip poplar.

Silently they took turns throwing in shovels of dirt, then stepped back while Warner, John, and Zedekiah completed the task. With tears in her eyes, Lizzie stuck the trunk of a small fir tree into the loose earth. No gravestone or marker was erected, only the scrawny, upright small conifer atop the mound of partially frozen sandy soil revealed my final earthly resting place.

Dad spoke the first words, "Georgie made our lives more interesting. Our family was stronger because of his presence, if only for a few years. Our world was a better place, if only a small part of it. That is all anyone can expect to accomplish on this earth."

Lizzie was the only other member of my family to utter any words at the burial. With low trembling voice she stated, "I'll forever remember this cold December day. When I'm sad and feeling sorry for myself, when I feel life is not worth living, I'll remember Little Georgie and his unfulfilled dreams. He will never be a great hunter or train a wolf pup. He will never write his life story. Someone else must write it for him."

By the end of December, snowdrifts along Sand Run reached two feet deep, making travel difficult. Dad and the older boys spent considerable time out in the weather, hauling hay and firewood. In contrast, Caroline, Daniel, and Emma seldom left the cabin. Lizzie went out to my grave every day, even in the harshest weather.

Life in the cabin seemed to change after my death. Of course, a major part of the change was associated with shortened day length— over fourteen hours of darkness. The last traces of daylight were fading by five o'clock. And not until seven the next morning did enough daylight return for the family to begin outdoor chores. Crowded cabin conditions and a diet consisting almost entirely of meat aggravated the somber mood.

One afternoon in December, while sitting in front of the roaring fireplace, Caroline suddenly proclaimed, "If we still lived in the Potomac Valley we would be visiting friends, or going to Romney, or attending a community sing right about now. Our relatives at Short Gap are probably planning a church social or even a barn dance."

No one responded.

The family's hens had quit laying eggs in December, and their cows were producing less than two gallons of milk each day. The last chestnuts were roasted over the fire in December. The last cabbage was eaten on New Year's day. The last turnip was eaten the middle of January, and the last winter squash the first week of February. The last of the flour was scooped from the bottom of the barrel before January ended, and the last cornmeal was baked in a skillet the third week of February.

From that point on, my family ate nothing but meat, supplemented with milk or hot tea brewed from twigs of balsam fir or sweet birch and dried teaberry leaves. Typically they ate fried bear sausages for breakfast, venison broth for lunch, and bear steaks for supper.

Although others grumbled, Caroline spoke up, "I know how you love hot biscuits, and I'm telling you now. I'm not spending another winter in this crowded, depressing little cabin if we can't store enough flour, cornmeal, and vegetables to last us till spring."

Daniel and little Emma shook their heads in agreement, but no one else said a word—notably not Dad.

Snows continued to fall throughout January and February, adding layer upon layer to the three-foot drifts that surrounded the cabin. The days might be getting longer but the snows were getting deeper.

One sunny day the last week of March, as melting snow dripped from the cabin roof, Lizzie came rushing into the cabin and announced, "Spring is here! There's no doubt now! I saw it with my own eyes. If you want to see come with me. And don't forget to bring one of our split oak baskets."

Caroline was receptive to any excuse that carried them out of the dark, dreary cabin, and hurriedly dressed the younger children. Lizzie led them to a north-facing hillside where the pointy leaves of several green plants had pushed their way up through the snow. The ramps were back!

Digging sticks brushed away the snow, leaf litter, and loose soil that provided a fertile seed bed for the onion-like ramps, and in no time the residual snow blanket was garnished with clusters of elongated green leaves perched atop bulbous white bases. The leaves were only three or four inches long, but the oniony bulb was nearly as large as it would grow that spring—about the size of the last joint on a person's little finger.

Their harvest only half-filled the oak basket that first day, but provided enough for everyone in the family to savor their first taste of spring greens. Caroline fried them in the heavy black skillet with one-inch thick bear steaks. The ramps did little more than tease the taste buds of my family, but everyone rambled nonstop about the bushels they would dig in coming weeks.

The same night my family enjoyed their first ramps of the spring, Dad announced, "I guess John and I'll be going to the Parsons settlement to trade our furs for badly-needed supplies. We need flour, cornmeal, sugar, salt, baking powder, gunpowder, and bullet lead. Think about what else you want."

I suspect that everyone slept soundly that night, comforted by dreams of hot biscuits and cornbread. Warner was disappointed that he could not go, but realized that he would be responsible for the safety of the rest of the family.

At breakfast the next morning, Caroline firmly stated, "We all need new leather boots, and certainly can use some cloth to sew new clothes. You boys may enjoy wearing deerskin shirts and pants, but the girls and I want something soft and comfortable."

While everyone else suggested items they wanted, but could live without, Lizzie solemnly confronted Dad, "Do you remember your promise to Mother as she was dying? She insisted you have a permanent stone marker placed on her grave—and that of each of her children. You promised! Now, you must have someone carve a gravestone for Georgie. You know we don't have the carving chisels to make one ourselves."

Dad nodded his head in the affirmative, but said nothing. Promises were easy to forget when you pray every night your family will survive the wilderness.

At supper that night, Dad surprised Lizzie by asking, "What should we have engraved on the stone?"

She immediately responded, "Georgie S. Leatherman. Born May 6, 1871. Died December 5, 1880. Such a short life. So much potential."

"That'll require a mighty big stone, and will most certainly cost quite a few furs to have it carved. But, I'll see what I can do," Dad answered.

The first week of April, Dad and John loaded the bundles of furs and dried ginseng onto Abe and Mack, and with a rifle in one hand

and a horse's reins in the other they trudged towards the southern end of Canaan Valley. They planned to visit with the Cosners and Freelands, and then the Nines before picking up the trail that headed west down to the Cheat River. They reckoned they would get to the Parsons settlement in three days, spend two days trading then spend three to four days on the return trip.

Buoyed by the promise of hot biscuits the day Dad and John returned, my family kept busy from daylight to dark. I still thought of them as my family, although I realized I would never again be a part of their lives. Much to my family's dismay, they woke on the fifth day following Dad and John's departure to nearly ten inches of fresh-fallen snow.

Eight days after they left, Dad and John returned to our cabin. Sacks of cornmeal and flour hung heavily across both horses' backs. Additional sacks bulged with the other items they had obtained in trade. The sweet fragrance of hot cornbread soon filled the cabin. Fried bear steaks and butter-soaked, cornbread were piled high on each plate that evening. For desert, pieces of cornbread were broken into bowls and half submerged in warm milk. It was the best meal my family had enjoyed since the previous November.

Lizzie solemnly spoke as the bowls were emptied, "Only one thing is missing from this feast—Little Georgie. By the way, Papa, where is Georgie's gravestone? I was so thrilled with the flour and cornmeal and cloth that I forgot about the stone."

With an awkward silence flooding the cabin, all eyes turned to Dad. He lifted his bowl and drank the last of his milk and cornbread before answering, "I ordered the gravestone from a carver, but he's so busy making stones for all those who died last winter that it won't be finished until June."

The valley slowly returned to life, as evidenced by the rosy hue and light green blush blanketing the mountainside, the bright green skunk cabbage in the swamps, the passage high overhead of honking Canada-bound geese, the high pitched calls of spring peepers, and the territorial calls of red-winged blackbirds. Tiny flowers of red maple and unfurling black cherry leaves proclaimed that winter was indeed over.

Marsh grasses greened up by the middle of May, and milk production from our Jersey cows increased dramatically. Livestock and members of my family began to regain the weight they had lost in winter.

With the promise of another growing season in the air, optimism returned to my family. Dad greeted the day with faith that the year's crops would be more than adequate to sustain the family through a long Canaan winter. His confidence was contagious, and the boys began clearing more land for crops.

In late April, seeds of cabbage, onions, beets, and buckwheat were pushed carefully into shallow soil between blackened stumps, with little attempt to make straight rows. Small sections of potatoes were planted in deeper rows. In the middle of May, squash seeds and tan, smooth beans were planted with yellow corn kernels.

But summer, and the associated growing season, does not truly arrive in Canaan until July. Dad had been warned about the likelihood of cold weather in June, but none of my family could believe the abrupt reappearance of cold weather the second week of June. A cold rain began falling early in the morning. It turned to slushy snow around midday, and continued until darkness arrived. The skies cleared quickly as the north wind pushed clouds away and brought Canadian air pouring into the valley.

The family awoke to a layer of ice in the water buckets sitting on the porch, and even a thin skim on the water bucket inside the cabin. Dad and the boys delayed breakfast until they had carried in several cherry logs and built a roaring fire in the fireplace. Wool coats were retrieved from their pegs where everyone had expected them to hang until October.

By the next afternoon the tender leaves of chestnut and maple trees were beginning to blacken. But most distressing of sights, the beans, squash, and corn were shriveled and lying flat on the ground. Even cabbage and potato sprouts were wilted.

In two days it was evident that the Leatherman garden would be a failure that summer. Those plants not killed would never mature before the first frost of autumn. Dad had been warned about the short growing season in Canaan, but never expected it to be less than sixty days. Without garden vegetables the family faced a winter just as bleak as the previous one.

Dad, the eternal optimist, told John they must leave for Parsons the next day to purchase more seed. He proclaimed, "If we hurry we can be back in less than a week, and can replant before the first of July."

Warner argued, "Maybe the replanted cabbage and squash and turnips and beets will mature, since they don't mind a little frost. But there's no way the corn and beans and potatoes will produce a crop. Also, we don't know if there's any seed left in Parsons."

After a short pause Warner continued, "None of us want to admit that we failed in making a home in the Canaan wilderness, but if we plan to spend the coming winter here we must be prepared to do so without vegetables for at least another year. We most likely will produce no garden this summer, and other than chestnuts, will be forced to depend on meat to survive the next fifteen months."

No one could refute Warner's prediction. A disturbing silence flooded the cabin. John, as second oldest son, felt he was old enough to venture an opinion and stated, "We have a tough decision to make. And unfortunately, we don't have much time to make it. We can make a hurried trip to Parsons and pray there are some seed potatoes and other garden seeds available, or we can set our minds to spending another winter here and do everything necessary to survive. We know we can shoot enough wild game to keep from starving. And we can harvest enough chestnuts to supplement the meat. We should have milk and eggs through the end of December. But…if we decide to leave Canaan and go back to the Potomac then we should leave as soon as possible. If we can get there by the first of July, we will have time to put out a late garden, and hopefully harvest beans and turnips."

At breakfast the next morning Dad announced, "John and I will leave for Parsons this morning. We'll return in one week. Pray that we find plenty of seeds to plant."

I couldn't determine if everyone prayed for seeds. I got the impression that some of my family did not want to spend another winter in Canaan. If that was true, they got their wish. Six days later, Dad and John returned—with no seeds to plant. My family's fate had been determined. They would certainly depart Canaan, and abandon the cabin, barn, cleared land, and me.

Dad and John had not returned empty handed. In one of the burlap sacks was my gravestone. Lizzie was so excited to see it that she began crying and announced, "Oh Papa, I'm so proud you got the gravestone. I'm certain Mom is relieved, also." As the stone lay on the ground, Lizzie read the inscription, "G. S. L., died Dec. 5, 1880, 9 y & 211 da."

Dad quietly spoke, "They didn't have room to spell out his name, or his birth date, or the phrase you wanted. They said the stone would have been so large we couldn't haul it back to Canaan unless we used a wagon."

Lizzie insisted they erect the stone at my grave that same day, and by evening my grave was prominently marked by the headstone and a smaller footstone. I was so proud to have a permanent marker erected to commemorate my life—the first gravestone in Canaan Valley.

Three days later my family left Canaan. The caravan resembled the one that had arrived a year earlier, with two obvious differences— it was headed south out of the valley, and it consisted of eight people rather than nine.

EPILOGUE

In the late 1990s, the hunter I referenced earlier garnered a deep, personal interest in the area around my gravestone, and my spirit is now confident he'll do everything possible to tell my story and install my family in the Canaan Valley annals. And most importantly, I'm confident he will do everything possible to see that my gravestone is preserved and remembered. It's even possible I might convince him to write about my biography—as Lizzie suggested.

Three different Brittany spaniels accompanied the man during the thirty-year period he was a regular visitor to Canaan Valley. I will forever remember one particular day in November 1999, when he was hunting with an orange and white Brittany named "Ruffee." Golden leaves of quaking aspen shimmered with each slight breeze. A cold front had swept through the previous night, leaving the sky a brilliant blue. A bright sun soon melted the silvery frost coating every goldenrod and spiraea plant and by early afternoon the hunter pulled off his long-sleeved shirt and stuffed it into his hunting coat.

Following a lunch break, during which hunter and dog shared two peanut butter sandwiches before taking a well-deserved nap in a soft moss bed, the hunt continued. The man directed Ruffee into a large stand of aspen cluttered with trees recently felled by the resident beaver family. It was too warm for a dog to hunt extended periods, but not so hot as to be stressful. Water was plentiful, providing the Brittany many opportunities to drink or plop down where the water was deep.

Ruffee was hunting about fifty yards downhill from her master, working her way along the top of a small bank that bordered one of the small tributaries of Sand Run. Suddenly she disappeared from sight as she went down over the bank. Her bell stopped ringing and the hunter reasoned she was lying in the water and resting. After less than thirty seconds a mental image of her on point a few yards from a crouching woodcock flashed through the hunter's brain. As he cautiously topped the bank where he had last seen her, he was shocked to see her lying awkwardly on her side with no signs of movement.

She was alive, but her breathing was shallow and erratic. After almost ten minutes she opened her eyes and lifted her head to stare at the hunter. But, even after an hour's rest, during which time she ate two dog biscuits and drank more water, she was unable to stand. They were nearly two miles from the pickup truck and she would need to be carried.

He realized that he could not carry both the double-barreled shotgun and the Brittany. They were less than 100 yards from my gravestone and the hunter quickly climbed the hill and hid his gun under a red spruce twelve paces east of the stone. I accompanied them as he carried his beloved dog to the truck.

The hunter quickly returned for his shotgun and hurried back to Ruffee. She weakly wagged her tail when he opened the truck's tailgate, but didn't lift her head. I watched the pickup fade out of sight as it splashed through mud holes lining the wood's road.

Four days later the hunter returned to my woods, but no frisky spaniel accompanied him. He had a small shovel slung over his shoulder and a large black plastic bag in his arms. Not far from my gravestone, at a site overlooking Sand Run, he began to dig. When the hole was two feet deep he discarded the shovel and lined the bottom of the hole with moss and leaves.

Satisfied with his efforts, he opened the plastic bag and gingerly slid out his dog. Gently lowering Ruffee into the grave, he ceremoniously added a worn leather collar, an empty shotgun shell, the wing of a ruffed grouse, and a faded hunting cap.

The hunter covered the dog with the plastic bag and then refilled the hole. He placed two small logs, overlapping to form a cross, across the grave.

I never saw the hunter with another dog, although he has visited my woods many times since. Every fall he returns, and after spending several minutes at his dog's grave he carefully examines my own gravestone. I can now transmeld my spirit thoughts with his on a consistent basis and have attempted to assure him that Ruffee's spirit now roams the woods near Sand Run. On several occasions he seemed to suspect her presence, but he has no way of knowing that her spirit looks forward to his return trips and joins him each time he returns.

The hunter spends so much time here that I often wonder about the possibility of his dying in this valley called Canaan. If that should happen, the hunter's spirit and Ruffee's spirit will surely join and the two of them can again roam Canaan Valley as a team. Even better, my spirit might join them, and our spirits could wander together. I would like that very much! Even spirits need friends.

CHRONOLOGY OF EVENTS

1835 — George W. Leatherman (GWL, the father) born in Hampshire County, WV.

1843 — Three elk killed on the Black Fork of Cheat River near Davis, Tucker County, WV (Maxwell 1898).

1857 — GWL married Mary Susan Whip.

1859 — Warner Washington born: 1st son.

1860–61 — Elk last reported in Canaan Valley (McWhorter 1915).

1861 — GWL Drafted into Confederate Army. Served less than one year then fled to Indiana with wife.

1862 — John William born in Indiana: 2nd son, 2nd child.

1862 — Leatherman family returned to Hampshire County.

1863 — West Virginia became a state on June 30.

1866 — Mineral County created from Hampshire County by Act of West Virginia Legislature.

1867 — Zedekiah Amos born: 3rd son, 3rd child.

1869 — Mary Elizabeth born: 1st daughter, 4th child.

1871 — George Sandford born: 4th son, 5th child.

1873 — Last recorded evidence of elk in West Virginia: tracks seen near the headwaters of Cheat River (McWhorter 1915).

1875 — Daniel Robert born: 5th son, 6th child.

1875 — Wife/Mother, Mary Whip Leatherman, died.

1876 — GWL remarried: Caroline Thrush.

1876 — GWL purchased nine tracts totaling 1,436 acres, previously owned by Adam Harness, at the Tucker County Sheriff's sale.

1878 — Emma Margaret born: 2nd daughter, 7th child of GWL. 1st child of Caroline.

1880 — The Leatherman family moved from their Hampshire County farm along the South Branch to Canaan Valley.

1880 — U.S. Census taker, Stuard S. Lambert, visited Canaan Valley in June.

1880 — George S. (the son) died: December 5.

1881–1884 — GWL moved his family to "…near W.VA C&P R.W." (Maxwell 1894).

1890 — The Leatherman family had moved again and lived in Mineral County, WV (U.S. Census, 1890).

1894 — A wolf was killed near St. George, Tucker County (Maxwell 1894).

1900 — A wolf was killed during January 1900 in Randolph County: the last record for West Virginia (Brooks 1911).

About The Author

Dr. Michael is a native West Virginian. He was born on Plum Run, in Marion County, near Mannington and Farmington, attended elementary school at Shinnston, and graduated from Magnolia High School in New Martinsville. He received a B.S. degree in Biology from Marietta College, and M.S. and Ph.D. degrees in Wildlife Ecology from Texas A&M University. He taught at West Virginia University from 1970 through 1997. Following retirement, he became a part-time resident of Canaan Valley and conducted numerous studies on the ecology of snapping turtles in that unique ecosystem. That research formed the basis for his historical novel, *A Valley Called Canaan: 1885-2002*. His fifty-year career as a wildlife biologist produced more than one hundred publications, both scientific and popular. Dr. Michael continues to be an active outdoorsman, researcher, and writer, concentrating his efforts on wildlife of the Appalachian Mountains. The most-recent product of this writing was his fascinating historical novel, *Shadow of the Alleghenies*.